THE LAPUTAN FACTOR

TRISTAN BLACK WOLF

ILLUSTRATIONS BY DREAM AND NIGHTMARE

authorHOUSE®

AuthorHouse™
1663 Liberty Drive
Bloomington, IN 47403
www.authorhouse.com
Phone: 1 (800) 839-8640

Published by AuthorHouse 05/28/2015

ISBN: 978-1-5049-1337-9 (sc)
ISBN: 978-1-5049-1336-2 (e)

Library of Congress Control Number: 2015908216

Print information available on the last page.

Any people depicted in stock imagery provided by Thinkstock are models,
and such images are being used for illustrative purposes only.
Certain stock imagery © Thinkstock.

This book is printed on acid-free paper.

Because of the dynamic nature of the Internet, any web addresses or links contained in
this book may have changed since publication and may no longer be valid. The views
expressed in this work are solely those of the author and do not necessarily reflect the
views of the publisher, and the publisher hereby disclaims any responsibility for them.

Dedications

From Tristan:

For William Windom, with fondness for years of
correspondence
and shared Mensa jokes. Miss ya, Bill.

From Night:

For all of my friends, family and people close to my heart.
Thanks for your support.
I could not have done this without you.

Acknowledgements

As always, M. Bradley Davis gets a nod of gratitude, a paw-shake of great appreciation, and a good chow-down, if we can manage to be in the same time zone at some point. (Thanks in particular for your advice about NIC cards, networking, and a few other technical details! I do occasionally suffer from imagination larger than my realm of knowledge, and you save me from myself in this instances.)

I very much thank those who read the early drafts of the book and made comments to help me out. (This includes humans and furs alike, so don't be surprised by some of the names!) I'm much obliged to you all: Dan Casbeer (who doesn't consider himself a furry, but in real life is rather fuzzy), Gabriel Clyde (a noble Australian Clydesdale and superlative author in his own right), Raul Greenscale (always up for a fresh "beta-reading" gig), Kittara Foxworthy (a vixen and author, with a great many good stories to her credit), Jybian Lawinde (a winged white tiger mage who's been hanging about with me for the past decade or so), Jon Sanders (a fine young otter), and Logan Womak (a handsome young Texas wolf of my acquaintance).

My splendid illustrator, Dream and Nightmare, actually inspired me to come up with this story. It started with a kind of "Wish You Were Here" postcard picture of his tiger character with another, as if the two were on vacation. I asked if I could write a short story – perhaps 2500-3000 words – about a vague idea that the picture inspired. About 47,000 words later...! No sense wasting a good novella, and even less sense not having it illustrated by one of the best furry artists in the world... so enjoy the words and pictures both. Much love to you, *Mein Mitternachtstiger...*

Another nod to the gentleman in my Dedication, as he's the actor noted for so many fine roles that I couldn't list them all. We met because of one of them – he was touring with his live one-man show of James Thurber's work, and I interviewed him for an article. From then on, William Windom and I started a lifelong correspondence, on and off, lasting over 30 years. His best known role in later years was his semi-regular appearance in the television series *Murder, She Wrote,* as Dr. Seth Hazlitt. In drawing the picture of the good doctor for this book, Night took a few features from Bill's overall appearance. I always thought Bill would make a good bear. Here was my chance to do so, borrowing a bit from the character that he brought to life so vividly.

And as always, my never-ending gratitude to the man who made me want to be a writer. Thank you, Ray Bradbury (1920 – 2012), for helping me unwrap and appreciate the gift of myself.

1

"Night?"

Sleepily, his eyes still closed, the large, muscular tiger shifted slightly and grunted, "Is that a noun, a farewell, or my name?"

"Night..."

"I'm gonna go with name."

"Night."

"Mm?"

"Where are you?"

A quick frown crossed the tiger's brow before it ran away again, afraid of waking the great beast fully. "I seem to be curled up next to a warm, well-formed, and inquisitive hyena." He pushed his muzzle lazily against his lover's side, sniffing softly, sighing. "A particularly nice-smelling if inquisitive hyena."

"Are you sure that's my scent, or is it yours?"

"They mix well."

For several long moments, the hyena made a great show of slowly licking and nibbling at the tiger's ears. Night stretched gently, eyes still closed, fighting the urge to purr, since he didn't want to give the game away too easily. It was a near thing; Donovan knew exactly what buttons to push, which was one of the reasons that their relationship had been building more steadily than most in Night's life. It's only natural to want more of what it is that makes you feel good. That thought took on a physical component, moving warmly through his body like a sweet, gooey sludge that seemed to bring various parts of him slowly more awake. Well, slowly in some places, more quickly in others.

The rough, wide tongue paused; Night could feel the warm breath in his ear, as the hyena whispered again, "Where are you?"

The tiger pressed his body up against his lover, eyes still closed, the tiger's head barely a dozen centimeters from the powerful hyena's. "Donovan, what are you talking about? I'm right here."

"Mitternachtstiger..." The canid's voice betrayed a great sadness; Night could sense his lover shake his head slowly. "Come back to me."

Night sat up sharply, his eyes snapping open, cursing. "What in—"

His breath caught in his throat as he looked around him. The room was familiar, even though he would swear that he'd never seen it before. Small, not cramped; "efficient" was perhaps the word, compact, organized, like a ship's cabin. He had no sensation of being on the ocean, and he couldn't see through the thick curtains across from the bed. His nose twitched, sniffing the air for clues to his surroundings, his ears pivoted forward like dual dish antennae, searching for sounds. A metallic smell, a touch of something like ozone, as if electricity crackled somewhere. It made his fur twitch. Sounds were minimal, hushed, distant, beyond well-insulated walls of some unknown material. He pushed the bedclothes away from his naked body; he shook his paws twice to get rid of them — he had to calm himself enough to retract his claws, peeking out at the end of his fingers just in case they were needed. The floor below his hindpaws felt strange, as if having a subtle vibration of some kind. He wasn't even entirely sure about the substance of the floor; it wasn't clear in the near blackness of the room, but he didn't want to risk a light just yet. A peek beyond the curtains first, figure out where he was.

He got more than a peek, although his mind could not yet process what he saw.

Above, below, all around him, an infinity of stars…

* * * * *

Night's ears splayed in shock, then pivoted sharply toward the door of the cabin as they locked in on something. Faint words, like an announcement onboard a ship. He couldn't make out the words, yet the tone seemed familiar, as if he'd been accustomed to hearing such announcements, like an aural carpet or background, something he'd learned to live with during his life aboard the star cruiser *Heartwielder.*

He shook his head. That bit of information had more or less simply appeared in his fevered brain, yet it had the feeling of being old news. *Heartwielder* was a flagship of the line, its own city in space, designed for transport, diplomatic hosting, and well-announced visits to various corners of the galaxy, with goodwill its intent and peaceful coexistence its hallmark. It also hosted a fleet of the most incredibly fast and surgically accurate single-pilot defense ships in the known sky, as well as the finest cadre of paramilitary fighter pilots ever assembled… of which he was one.

As if being put on alert for an upcoming mission, the tiger felt something ripple through him, tip to toes, his muscles feeling as if they had suddenly been reprogrammed to the purpose of flying a Starhawk-class fighter ship at top speed, space-stitching through enemy fire to deliver one hit – for one was all that was needed to disable the target, destroy it if required – and escape through the remaining wave of exploding energy and debris to rise back again into the eternal darkness of space, yet another mission accomplished without error or defensive casualty.

Forepaw to his head, Night reeled, fell back to sit on the bed once more. What was all this? Where was it coming from? This was his life, he remembered. It was memory, it was all his own experience and memory, just as he had lived it for these past two and a half decades and change, all of his experience, all of his training, learning, doing, accomplishing, all that he could remember, this was his life.

And he knew nothing at all of it until a few moments ago.

A soft chime announced itself inside the cabin. "Lieutenant Kovach… wake-up call for Lieutenant Kovach… please report to General Briefing in 30 minutes."

"Acknowledged." The word was out of Night's muzzle before he could stop it, as if from habit of long standing. The chime and the announcement ceased. "Lights, half." From unknown and virtually unseen sources, mild light illuminated what he could only think of as his cabin. *Kovach.* His mind told him that the name was his, yet it wasn't. Or it didn't used to be, or something like that. His name was… was…

The tiger breathed deeply. His eyes focused, and everything fell into place. He had time for a shower before the briefing. There should be food and drink there; this was a scheduled conference, not an emergency scramble. That could happen before long, because there was some tension here in the borderlands, but it wouldn't be a problem. For today, preparation, instruction, drill if necessary – the basics, always good to practice. Meanwhile, it wouldn't do to be late.

Lieutenant Ambrose Bierce Kovach rose from his bed and got his day started.

2

The briefing was good, meaning short and to the point. Gorgonea Tertia was not exactly one of the top stars in everyone's constellation list, but there were some reports from that general region that might indicate some trouble for travelers going within a short distance of the place. A contingent of Starhawks was to check out the area and report back; orders were strictly recon, no contact and no engagement unless exclusively defensive. Preferred result of hostile contact was called Plan Killdeer, named after the Earthly bird that feigns being injured in order to lure a predator far away from the nest, then escapes at the last moment. The slight variation here was to lure the predator back to the predetermined rendezvous point, where the rest of the fleet would seem quietly to appear from nothingness, to give the predator cause for second thoughts, and quite likely cause for a change of underwear.

Kovach was to be part of this team of six, designation Snake Lady, with the call code Medusa, in honor of the most famous of the gorgons. He was to be Medusa Six, covering everyone's tail – a job he knew how to do very well indeed. He met up with his contingent at the SimCenter shortly after the briefing. It made sense to warm up a bit before going out in the deep cold of space.

Outside of the simulation complex, a grizzled bulldog chomped on a conspicuously unlit cigar and stared at the half-dozen furs in front of him. "Line up, you pups; it's not like you've never done this before."

The others grinned, making themselves stand more to attention, tails still, eyes and ears forward, showing the discipline of trained pilots who were ready to calm down and show more respect to Sgt. Sumner, the old "top dog" of the Starhawks. No one knew what his real rank was; he had been "the Sarge" for so many years now, training and honing squad after never-ending squad of pilots, that he was occasionally referred to as Drill Instructor Emeritus. He had been, still was, and would always be called "Sarge." His command of respect didn't rely on mere rank. As the six Medusans gathered themselves, Kovach snapped into position with the rest of them, knowing that he'd done this many times before, some part of him knowing that he hadn't.

"Sound off, Snake Lady. Medusa One."

"Lentz," a sleek black panther answered crisply. He'd worked hard to get where he was, and no team had a better squad leader, even if he was by-the-book more than the job warranted. He made up for it in loyalty to his team.

"Medusa Two."

"Tolliver." A tall, muscled white German shepherd who looked as if he might not even fit into the small main cabin of a Starhawk. Standing nearly two full meters in height, the gentle giant was more likely to stop a fight by simply catching a flying fist rather than throwing one of his own.

"Medusa Three."

"Perryman." A lean, hard-looking lop-eared rabbit who sometimes sported an eye patch, and carried with him something of a reputation. The eye patch concealed an extremely advanced cybernetic scanner/sensor and micro-computer that presumably connected directly into the hare's brain, providing more information than any ordinary eye could, and doubling as an expression of bad-ass-ness.

"Medusa Four."

"Rains." Another tiger, like Kovach, about the same general build, perhaps several centimeters shorter, and white instead of orange tawny. A Brit of sensitivity, cordiality, and an unrepentant fondness for the raw violence of a rugby match with a drunken referee, or its pub-crawling equivalent. It was, in a way, ironic that he was a key part of a force designed to be merely disabling rather than crippling. He preferred to think of it as a means of making new friends who he could later meet on the field – preferably head-first.

"Medusa Five."

"Baptiste." A Husky with traditional markings, including the heterochromic eyes (one golden brown, one clear blue) of the purebred; strong, feisty, a good dozen centimeters shorter than Kovach… and female. No one could say that she slept her way to the top. No one dared, after what happened in that one incident with the formerly-male bovine. Contrary to rumor, there was no dull spoon, although that might have been less painful.

"Medusa Six."

"Kovach."

"Well damn if they didn't get themselves in the right order," the bulldog grumbled, cocking his chin toward a door in the bulkhead that sighed open as he spoke. "Designation's on each chamber. Pick the right door, set up, jack in, you know the routine. SimRun designation Phibriglex-62. We'll boot you up. Get moving before I boot yer tails."

The chambers were in designation order; Kovach took up the one nearest the bulkhead door. The pilot's chair faced him as he entered. He spun, sat in the chair, found the primary controls and entered the required initial sequences as he settled his tail into position and pivoted the chair back toward the main console and viewport. Detaching the red personal pin drive from the lanyard around his neck, he jacked into the primary data 'corder, ready to record his every move. His fore and hind paws moved automatically, checking sensors, touch-plates, joysticks, keypads, and other controllers. Lights and screens came up at his command; the boards hummed with power, pinging and chiming with soft positive acknowledgements as the full power of the control systems came online.

"Voice command," Kovach spoke clearly.

The automated system responded softly, in a precise BRP that always made Night wonder if Rains had something to do with the programming. "Designation."

"Medusa Six."

"Identification."

"Kovach, Delta-Echo-Bravo niner seven niner Omega."

"Initializing voice command. Please speak."

"My hovercraft is full of eels."

The systems hummed for a moment. The voice, upon its return, sounded almost disappointed. "Insufficient phonemes; please continue."

"Drop your panties, Sir William, I cannot wait until lunchtime."

Another pause. "Phonemes accepted. Voice command ready."

"Kovach," drawled Sumner in the tiger's headset, "you have a strange taste in comedy."

"Yet you recognized it, Sarge."

"Call the Church Police." A click in Kovach's ear told him that the Sergeant had switched to the general channel. "Okay, pups, kits, and others, get ready for synch. Systems up."

A squeal in the headset made Kovach cringe. When it finally had diminished, he heard Perryman pipe up, "All this money spent on these sim systems, and you can't figure out what makes that horrible noise?"

"We can figure it out, Medusa Three; we just love yankin' yer chain. Cut the chatter. We've got a nice set of chain-yankin' ready for you, starting with simulated launch. Hope you didn't have anything slimy for breakfast, or you're likely to see it again." Sumner continued in official voice, for the simulated black boxes and anyone else who might be listening; Starhawk simulations were a good source of entertainment on the *Heartwielder*. "Snake Lady Simulation, Phibriglex-62, launch in three, two, one…"

The word "simulation" was an understatement. Even though he knew that he really wasn't going anywhere, Kovach's stomach lurched as the screens imitated movement and the entire chamber itself rumbled and pulsed as if he really were being launched at full ignition speed – something that pulled a couple of gees out of him, or as some of the male pilots sometimes said, turned their sheaths into "innies."

The tiger let his breath out as the simulation settled into the feel of normal space travel. In a lot of ways, the launch was the worst; after that initial acceleration, the rest was easily handled by inertial dampeners. The chatter in Kovach's ears was normal, each ship checking in. He said his piece when required, all very routine. "Keep it by the numbers, folks." The bulldog's grumbling voice kept things in order. "Follow the bouncing ball."

An artificial target appeared on screen. Lentz, Medusa One, took the lead as the others held formation. The panther talked his way through the routine – intercept, identify, contact, respond. In this case, the target identified itself, satisfied Lentz of his creds, and was escorted quite peacefully for a short distance before he disengaged and returned to formation. "Not much fun in that, Sarge," he said playfully.

"Careful what you ask for."

Another target appeared onscreen, and Tolliver went after it. Shortly after contact, the target vessel made a quick change in course. Lentz ordered Perryman into position (despite Tolliver's insistence that he could handle it), and the two of them executed some very nice pincer ploys to get the target to submit. Although the target showed weapons power-up, it backed down after the two Medusans erected shields and readied their defensive weapons – just enough firepower to disable. The target vessel bolted for the borderlands; Lentz ordered the ships back. "This is only simulation, guys; let's leave the chase for when we need it."

"Medusa One, this is Five," Baptiste piped up. "Target ship has a strange radiation signature in its engines. Something is off about this…"

"Nice catch, puppy," Sumner grumbled into his headset. Kovach made adjustments of his own, in case he would be needed.

"Medusa One confirming. Tolliver, Perryman, continue on back like nothing is happening. Medusa Six, what've you got?"

Kovach checked several readouts and made some calculations. "Target has some sort of jump capability."

"No freakin' way," Tolliver barked. "Engine configuration shows—"

"—that we've been suckered," Baptiste announced, speaking quickly. "Guys, I think we've found one of those stolen Bradbury engines we heard about last month."

Lentz's voice positively crackled. "Snake Lady, break to full intercept, start with Alpha pattern, we'll wing it from there."

Kovach reacted instantly, falling out of position at a speed of point-five and assuming a space-stitch pattern that kept him available to the squad but far enough back to make him a secondary target. "Move out, Baptiste, I've got your tail."

"Not what I heard," Perryman quipped.

"Offering yours?" Kovach shot back.

"Kill the chatter, furs," Lentz growled. "Target is accelerating. Baptiste, give me a reading, has he got the four-five-one charging?"

"Affirmative, Medusa One." The Husky's voice was clipped and all business. "Six, can you confirm?"

"That would be a yes," the tiger's voice radiated calm despite the tingling nerves and rapid movements of his forepaws across the complicated console.

"Medusa Four, where'd you go?" Lentz asked the air.

"Time for elevenses, people," came the white tiger's British accent. Kovach looked up from his tactical screens to the viewport, just in time to see that Rains' Starhawk had accelerated to point-seven or better and swooped in front of the target vessel from its eleven-o'clock position and cut downward toward the five, then away again as the target fired feebly at the place where the Medusan had been.

"What the hell…!" Lentz exclaimed.

"My wake should help disrupt the field build-up for several seconds. Bought some time."

"Snake Lady," Lentz growled, using the short form for the squad collectively, "arm disabling weapons. Let's bring this idiot down."

"Medusa Five," Baptiste cried out, "Snake Lady, disengage weapons! Repeat, *disengage!*"

Kovach caught the mistake even as Lentz tried to sputter his instructions to the team. "Confirmed!" the tiger shouted. "Jump field forming, and it's... I don't know what to call it, the damned thing is..."

Baptiste cut in. "Break off, repeat, break off – the field is causing local spatial disruption, we can't get caught in it or..."

"I've got his shield generators," Perryman shouted, "we can take them down, we can..."

"No time! The jump field is..."

Kovach saw a bright flare from some corner of the screens, as if someone had fired on the target ship, but that was impossible, who could be stupid enough... The flare struck the target ship, and everything seemed suddenly to slow down, images jigging on the screen as if something wasn't entirely right, as if space had decided not to work correctly, pixel-corrections in splats and edges as if the program were glitching in the simulation (this was a simulation, wasn't it, not a real mission?), and as if to prove that a simulation could be just as real as anything else, the tiger felt himself smacked in the head by a volleyball, and he fell down into hot sand, his eyes shutting instinctively against the burning bright sun in the sky. Voices, laughing, smell of sea air, and someone's paws carefully checking his head, a voice saying, "You okay, buddy? You looked about a million klicks away when that ball hit you!"

The tiger opened his eyes and saw a hyena, a sweetly smiling hyena, gazing at him with deep concern.

"...Donovan?"

3

The hyena laughed gently. "Looks like you had your furniture rattled a little, tiger. Think you can sit up?"

Carefully accepting the helping paws, the tiger moved into a sitting position on the hot sand, trying to check his flight suit for... His paw touched his muscular, cream-furred chest, moved toward his head – no headset, no flight suit, just bathing trunks, nothing... His tail lashed suddenly against the sand, and the hyena looked at him worriedly.

"Night? Are you okay?"

Night. Like a nickname? Or a name. *His* name, except that his name was ... his name was Lieutenant... He looked up into the hyena's face again. *Donovan.* The hyena's name was Donovan. He wasn't part of the Snake... the what? *Snake...* From tip to toes, something rippled through him, made him cry out just once, a barking sound of surprise, or shock, or a gasping of breath.

"Night?" The hyena knelt next to the tiger, his paws upon shoulders, shaking gently. "Night, talk to me, are you all right? Are you choking? Can you breathe all right?"

Finally, the tiger managed to put a paw to his lover's arm. "Okay," he said shakily, "I'm okay, just... think I got the wind knocked out of me or something." He looked around himself quickly, seeing other furs watching, the others they were playing volleyball with, the other guys that they'd met down here on the beach, the slim, nimble otter who jumped as if air were like the water he swam in so gracefully, and the tall, well-formed giraffe (said he was an artist, maybe?), and the lithe young Malaysian pup with the never-ending smile, and the brown-furred wolf with the shoulder-length black headfur and orange Hawaiian shirt, watching from the sidelines. The tiger was remembering, *remembering* that he and Donovan were on vacation together, that this happy summer beach was the reward for a long period of testing at work, a big project, finally on its way to being finished, and this was the long-awaited break. Two full weeks of sun, sand, surf, and with Donovan in the picture, no doubt another short "s-word" in the sweet summer nights. If there's one thing Night knew after all these months with the hyena, it was that the pup did love his lovemaking.

Something in the tiger's mind reached outward, as if flipping back through the pages of a well-loved book, and he remembered his two and a half decades and change of growing up in a Midwestern city, going to school, getting his degree, working on certifications and Masters-level classes, getting his job, doing his work, living in his apartment, with Donovan having nearly moved in, they were getting along so well together, and the project and the vacation, all of the years, the people, the memories…

Night shook his head. Points for style, after all; he was a cat, mustn't let himself look bad in front of everyone else. "Maybe I need to get out of the heat for a little while." He smiled as he stood up and faced the hyena. "A nice cooling shower, perhaps. Wanna scrub my back?"

Donovan grinned back. "That's not usually the way I'm facing, but I'm adaptable."

"WTMI!" bemoaned one of the other volleyballers. "Hell, not enough!" cried another. A third chimed in with "Can I run the camera?" The wolf watched, said nothing.

Laughing, the hyena took the tiger's paw and led him back to their room at the resort. "Thanks for the game, guys! We'll catch you later!"

"You've already caught one!" came the last jeer, and the game began to find a new start with the various males already in the area. This was the "gay side" of the beach, Night remembered. Lots of eye candy, and no one minded the casual flirt, much less the audacious proposal. A more fun crowd to play with, so to speak.

"Are you sure you're all right?" Donovan asked softly, still watching Night carefully.

The tiger chuckled. "It'll take more than a smack in the head with a volleyball to take me down, puppy," he said affectionately. "Delayed stress response, eh? Still haven't shaken the job out of my head yet."

"No talking about work," Donovan said in mock severity. "Break the rules, and I'll send you to supper without bed."

"A horrible fate, to be sure!" Night opined.

They got to their room just in time; another few seconds longer, and the hyena might have started stripping in the hallway. As it was, they made it to the shower quickly enough to escape any potential charges of public indecency. Sand was washed away, backs were scrubbed, and other exercises were conducted which reassured both parties that all systems were in perfect working order. Between that and the volleyball, it was a toss-up (pardon the pun) as to which workout was more aerobic. Finally getting back to bed, they lay in each other's arms, letting their breathing slow and become normal again.

"So," Night murred into the hyena's sensitive ear, "think I'm suffering any residual brain damage?"

"No pain where there's no sense." Donovan giggled as Night tickled him mercilessly for nearly half a minute. "Okay, okay! I give!"

The tiger took him back into his arms. "Yes, you do, and very well, may I add."

"Why, thank you, Mr. Tiger sir." The hyena wriggled happily in Night's embrace, then sobered a little. "Are you really okay, luv?"

"You're a worry-wart."

"An anxious pimple? Ew!" Donovan grinned briefly. "Look, it's me who watched over you when you were in hospital those several days. So I'm going to keep worrying."

Night sighed with only slightly exaggerated exasperation. "They wouldn't have let me go if they weren't sure I was okay. Besides, they had to soak the insurance as much as they possibly could; if they didn't make a big profit, they'd lose their hospital license. Or at least their stock-holders."

Tenderly, the hyena stroked the tiger's long dark brown headfur. "Night... it scared me. You were in a coma for nearly two days. I was freaked out of what few spots I've got, and I don't ever want to get that close to losing you ever again. I know you're not ready to commit – we've had that conversation, and I won't push – but I really do want to be with you, quite possibly forever. I love you, and therefore I'm going to worry about you." He grinned. "So get used to it."

"Well, for what it's worth, spotty-britches, I happen to be rather fond of you too. And it wasn't a coma."

"Do I have to show you the hospital reports?"

Night shook his head. "It was just stress."

The hyena's ears splayed enough to make it look as if he were about to unleash a vicious growl. "Don't apologize for those bastards."

"I'm not apologizing for anyone. It was just stress at work, that's all…"

"It was that damned project, and I don't want to talk about it right now." Donovan rolled over to face away from the tiger, as if to slam the lid on the subject. The tiger hesitated, knowing well his lover's famous temper and his opinions of the particular workplace in question. He reached out to apologize. The young male grumbled, but didn't object further as Night pulled him close again.

"Donovan, I'm sorry. Didn't mean to put a kink in your tail." He nibbled the hyena's neck gently. "You've got enough kinks already."

"It's got to stop."

"What's got to stop?"

"I'm serious, Night," the hyena said to the air in front of him, so softly that the tiger almost didn't hear. "There's something wrong about that place."

"What do you mean?"

"I don't want you to go back."

"What?"

"Go back."

"I can't hear you."

"Kovach."

"What?"

"Kovach, snap out of it. Wake up."

The tiger's eyes whipped open. The ceiling above him was metallic, the air around him different, too dry, almost crackling. No beach smell, no ocean smell; some sweat, some chemicals like disinfectants, unguents, ointments, something electric.

"I think he's coming around."

The voice was familiar, yet... He squeezed his eyes against his will, screwed them up tightly, felt a ripple course through from tip to toes, fought the sensation briefly, fought to remember what the beach smelled like (what beach?), what the hyena smelled like (what... you mean Tolliver? Completely different type of pup...). He grunted as the rippling came through again, stronger, like being poured through a filter, like being pressed through a wringer, like...

Lieutenant Kovach snapped his eyes open and saw Sumner's bulldog face hovering almost too close.

"Back among the living, Kovach?"

4

"What happened?"

"Simulation glitch." The bulldog chewed on his unlit cigar. Kovach wondered how big a supply the Sarge had; he was never without the damned things, and they never looked any shorter. "Nothing bad, but the feedback seems to have knocked a few of you senseless. Tolliver and Perryman are in the next couple of beds. You're the first one to wake up."

"How bad?"

"Talk to the sawbones." Sumner started to move away. "I'll go check on the other two."

Kovach lay still and concentrated on breathing. Something still wasn't right. He tried to think back to the simulation, to what had happened. Sarge had thrown a big monkey wrench into the works, which was sound training methodology, but something had gone wrong. Something about the Bradbury engines. He had read about the theft last month; everyone in the cadre had – it was a huge deal, a genuine game-changer. The four-five-one engine created a warp field that literally folded space. The ship inside the field was fine, but anything around the ship for a radius of about a half-dozen klicks was "folded" – matter was taken out of three dimensional space and dropped into two or even one dimensional space. This folding released energy as the stray matter – usually just hydrogen atoms, in open space – was forced into a completely incompatible dimension. It was as if the ship inside the field was able to slip through a fourth dimensional hole by forcing the stuff around it into a two dimensional space. That wasn't a scientifically correct explanation, but it was close enough for descriptive purposes.

Folding a hydrogen atom wasn't too big a bang – a comparative firecracker. Several dozen around the ship when it utilized the warp made quite a nice show of fireworks. This is where the designation of the engine came from; the inventor's name really was Bradbury, and some far distant ancestor of his was a writer with a fascination for book-burnings, and paper ignited at 451°F. Nothing like a literary reference to make science more interesting.

However, anything else in the way of the field creation – any matter at all, be it living or non – was flattened to a thickness of none-whatsoever. The larger the chunk of matter, the more powerful the explosions, none of which affected the ship inside the field since, to make a bad joke, it had a perfect alibi – it wasn't there at the time. Quite literally, it was both somewhere and somewhen else.

Kovach thought it over. What if the simulation had been too accurate? What if the computers tried to simulate what happened when something big got caught in the formation of the four-five-one field? Something big, or even something small, if it were powerful enough, something like…

…*a plasma shuriken.*

The Starhawks were equipped with weapons that were designed not for maximum destruction, like conventional attack weapons; these were designed for short, sharp, disabling attacks for defensive purposes. *Heartwielder* stood by its mission: Peace in the Galaxy, to put it briefly. They dealt with aggression not by destroying it but by shutting it down. The plasma weapon created for the Starhawks was so compact, so small, and so precise that the pilots had taken to calling them by the name given to a throwing weapon used by exceptionally skilled assassins of ancient times.

Powerful enough to penetrate shields of energy or physical matter, the plasma shuriken could disable engines, weaponry, and navigational systems in seconds, yet by itself was non-lethal to living flesh. In some process that Kovach didn't have the science to understand, the shuriken would cut through steel plating like a scalpel, yet upon reaching the targeted system, it dispersed into an electromagnetic pulse that shorted out the systems with no direct damage to flesh. It behaved like a pill with a coating that bypassed the stomach so that the medicine was absorbed in the upper intestines. Not a pretty image, perhaps, but one that worked.

Kovach had no idea how much power the damned thing had, nor what would happen to it if it were suddenly two-dimensional. Had Tolliver fired a shuriken into the field, against orders?

"How many fingers am I holding up?"

The tiger looked toward the voice. "Yours, or someone else's?"

"Responses like that get pilots stricken from flight lists for days at a time," the old bear grumped at him. He took out a pen light and moved it toward Kovach. "You want your eyes testin'," he said in a "down east" accent that spoke of his having spent years in the area of Maine, down on Earth. The natives still kept their accents carefully honed. "Keep those baby blues focused on the center of my forehead."

The sawbones moved the light across Kovach's eyes a few times, speaking to the air. "Review of Systems – HEENT, possible contusion behind left ear, negligible; cardiovascular, negative; respiratory, negative; GI, neg... hell, the whole panel is negative, so note it. Well-developed adult feline male, and stop looking at me like that, Kovach, it's a medical term, presenting (no not like that) after episode of unconsciousness secondary to unknown trauma during Starhawk simulation run. BP 108/70, pulse regular at 58, respirations calm at 12, oximetry 97% on ship's air. Speaking in full sentences, or at least as much as a pilot can manage. Lungs clear; heart S1, S2, no murmur, rub, gallop, heave, or thrill.

Yes, tiger, the thrill is non-existent, at least for me. Abdomen soft, no rebound, guarding, or tenderness. Neurologically intact, despite apparently having that thing in his skull laughingly referred to as a brain being rattled around a bit. No evidence of concussion, physical, mental, neurological, or otherwise." The doctor nodded, clicked the light off.

"Do I pass inspection, Dr. Hazlitt?"

"You aren't dead, blind, or handicapped, so what the hell are you doing in my sick bay?"

"Taking up valuable space."

"Ayuh, ya are. Back to your cabin, rest a while, no action till tomorrow, and that includes anything that requires intense physical activity, so keep your pecker in your pants." Hazlitt raised his eyebrows. "Not that I expect you to take my advice, but I'd be remiss in my duties if I didn't at least try."

Kovach swung his legs over the side of the examination table and stood up. "Hey doc, got a question."

"Not my type, tiger-boy."

"Not what I was going to ask. Baptiste has your eye, if I'm not mistaken."

"She has both of them, actually."

"I've had a weird symptom lately, not sure about it. Not even sure how to describe it, but…"

"I don't recall seeing hypochondria in your chart, Kovach. Spit it out."

The tiger paused. "Have you ever heard of someone… well, rippling?"

The bear raised one eyebrow to express something just short of sarcasm. "Stippling, yes, like a rash. Crippling, like an accident, or even nippling, which is something I do to make a female call out my name, repeatedly. What the hell is rippling?"

Kovach started to form an answer and realized that he had no idea what he was talking about. "Maybe just blood pressure. You know, like getting dizzy if you sit up too fast."

"Your blood pressure is fine, which means you don't need any drugs to enhance your performance, which the grapevine says is pretty good. Now get your tail out of here, and take the rest of you with it."

"Aye-aye, doc." Kovach snapped off a mock salute and a grin, giving the sawbones a good reason to snarl and go elsewhere. The tiger gathered his blue pin drive and a few other belongings from the table next to the bed and stepped out of the curtained alcove and looked to his left, where two other examination tables held the white Shepherd and the rabbit, both seeming to come slowly back to consciousness. They were in good paws for now; he would catch up with them later. Right now, his goal was food; it had been some time since breakfast.

As he left the sick bay, Kovach heard his name called. Turning, he found Baptiste running up to join him. "Are you all right?"

"Medically sound, at least." He looked sideways at her as they walked, his ears twitching in what might be called embarrassment in someone with less ego. "I should probably thank you. I don't know what went on in the simulation, but I can't help but think it would have been worse if you hadn't caught on to the Bradbury engine."

The Husky looked away, a smile on her muzzle. "I was just surprised to see it in a simulation. It's very recent news, all things considered. I wouldn't have thought they'd have programmed anything for it this quickly."

"That's something I'd like to ask you." Kovach looked around quickly, covertly, to make sure their conversation was at least reasonably private. "What did you think about the simulation?"

"Meaning?"

"What happened in there? Was it a glitch, a programming error, what? Why is it that three of us got physical injuries from it?"

Baptiste imitated Kovach's look around. "Had lunch?"

The tiger paused, saw the look in the Husky's eyes, and said, "No, not yet. Heading to the mess, if you'd like to join me."

"Glad to."

5

Heartwielder was huge, as much a city as any land-based city. Quite apart from administrative facilities, housing, and other required support, it boasted four promenade areas, each including restaurants. For the paramilitary, another option was a mess hall that was more like an all-hours cafeteria and grill. Some civilians enjoyed it as well, if only for the thrill of chowing down near the celebrity-like Starhawk pilots, or for the amusement of dining in an establishment called This Is A Mess.

Kovach filled his tray with a bit more food than he might have done ordinarily. The events of the morning had made him hungry. He and Baptiste flashed their blue pin drives at the register (in the mess, pilots' meals were comped directly) and sought a table in a quiet corner. It was past the peak lunch period for the ship, so the place was comparatively empty. They each took several bites from their various selections, made desultory conversation, until they felt sure no one was tuning in on them.

"What do you remember?" Bapiste asked abruptly.

The tiger swallowed his food, using the time to think about the question. "I've been trying to piece it together. I suppose I should review the pin drive to—"

"It won't be there."

"What?"

"This morning's drill has been redacted. General order from above. All of our pins were still jacked in when the call was made. Lentz, Rains, and I weren't allowed to touch the drives; we were taken from the pods, told to wait, and handed our pins before we left. We were told that the simulation had a glitch that revealed a program vulnerability, so they redacted the entire simulation from the pins in case of a security breach."

Kovach considered. "Sensible enough precaution."

"If that's what it was."

"What do you mean?"

"It was more than a glitch." The Husky's eyes were hard. "Three of us had a physical reaction – actual physical damage. That's supposed to be impossible. Even if we were neuro-linked, there shouldn't have been physical damage."

"What are you talking about?" The tiger frowned. "I was knocked unconscious, yes, probably a sensory overload. Felt like being hit in the head, but I wasn't actually hit."

"You got the least of it. Tolliver was in the lead. He was treated for burns."

"Electrical fire?"

"Radiation."

Kovach's fork stopped halfway to his muzzle. "There's no radioactive source anywhere near—"

"Except for the Bradbury Drive."

He dropped his fork and stared at her. "It was a simulation, Baptiste. It was nothing but a bunch of screens and data and special effects. It's a video game on steroids and a military budget. It wasn't real."

"No," she said, looking down at her plate. "It wasn't real. How could it have been?"

Long seconds passed. The tiger only stared at her, his tail lashing behind him like some kind of biological lie detector informing him that he wasn't telling the truth himself. His voice was quiet. "I haven't known you that long, but I don't think you're the type to go crazy. Just to make sure – you do know how nutty that sounds, right?"

"Oh, hells yeah." The Husky managed a smile. "That's the fun part about redacted documents – you can pretend that they originally said anything you want them to."

"If I go back to sick bay and pester Doc Hazlitt, is he going to tell me that Tolliver had radiation burns, or something else?"

Baptiste snorted, a wry grin on her muzzle. "Probably something else. The one you'll want to talk to is Perryman."

The tiger waited for her to continue, then the idea fell in place. "His eye."

"I think he saw more than the rest of us combined; that cyberoptic implant has a helluva range."

"No question." Kovach managed to get some more food into him. "All right, let's play the What Ifs. The simulation could have had a glitch; it could have been improperly programmed; or maybe it was programmed too well. Whatever's behind it, the question remains – how did a programmed simulation cause physical damage?"

The Husky smiled between bites. "You make it sound like it reached out and slapped you."

(smacked in the head by a volleyball)

"I remember a physical sensation," Kovach said carefully, not sure where the thought had come from. "But unless you see any bruising, then nothing actually hit me. It's Tolliver I'm thinking of. What makes you think it was a radiation burn?"

"I only caught a glimpse, and I heard a medtech say something." She shook her head slowly. "I know I didn't imagine it. I thought about it carefully, trying to separate the simulation from real life. In the sim, there could have been some flashback from the Bradbury Drive if it were damaged."

"From a shuriken?"

She nodded. "But I don't know who would have been stupid enough to fire one at a charging four-five-one, not in real life anyway."

Kovach thought of the pin drive, remembered what she'd said about it being redacted. "We only have our own memories to rely on, and I'm not sure how reliable mine might be."

"Glad I'm not the only one."

The tiger pushed his tray aside. "Let's find Perryman."

* * * * *

The pilots caught up with the rabbit in his quarters, since he was told by Doc Hazlitt to "put those damned big paws up and rest" for the remainder of the day. If not for the fact that said orders were on his electronic record as well (if couched in more acceptable medical terms), Perryman would have been working out in the gym; unfortunately for him, his pin drive denied him entry to anything but the hydrotherapy pool or the sauna. Kovach and Baptiste found the restless pilot working up a sweat with his own set of free weights. It was Perryman's way to shrug off tension, irritation, even the odd dollop of hostility that wasn't usually part of the rabbit's nature, and it would take more than orders from the CMO to stop him from exercising himself into a singular need for a shower. The Husky discreetly wrinkled up her nose when she entered the cabin; conversely, the tiger's nose relayed a signal that made Kovach wish that the rabbit were on the menu for dessert. He shoved the idea away and focused on what they came for.

"Your pins redacted too?" Perryman panted from beneath his triceps curls – a form guaranteed to expose one's armpits to the rest of the room. Inwardly, Kovach grinned.

Baptiste nodded. "Were you close to Tolliver when you were taken to sick bay?"

"Close enough." The lop panted through a few more reps. "That was no electrical burn."

"What did you see?"

The dumbbell passed from one paw to the other, giving the other armpit a chance to express itself, which it did with olfactory eloquence. "With the real eye or the good eye?"

"Make us happy and give us both," the tiger quipped.

"Ain't about to make you happy, stripey-butt."

"You already have." Kovach made a show of sniffing the air. "Fresh-baked testosterone. All I need is some juniper berries." In spite of herself, Baptiste chuckled.

Perryman slammed the dumbbell to the deck, making a noise that could probably be heard all the way to the sick bay. "If you weren't such a hot-shot pilot..." The rabbit grabbed a towel from its rack and used it to wick away what perspiration he could. "Be good, and I might give you this as a consolation prize."

"Oh, and how wonderfully consoled I would be." The tiger grinned at the lop, who gave in and smiled as well.

"What I saw was strange, for many reasons." Perryman relaxed his posture a little, even though Kovach noticed the hare's fur twitch a little, as if in response to a cool breeze, or an unwelcome memory. "Visually, the burn looked bad – second degree at least, lost some fur and some of the skin underneath. Nothing lethal by any stretch, but I can bet it didn't feel good. It was the pattern that I noticed first."

"Pattern?" asked the Husky.

"Almost like a stylized arrow, something curving, with some kind of lettering."

"Tell me you're kidding."

"It's what I saw. In fact, I can do you one better." He rose and padded to his computer terminal, sat down to activate it, then seemed to think better of the idea. He flicked a switch to one side. An all-too-familiar synthetic voice inquired, "Confirm shut down?"

"Confirmed," Perryman said, adding superfluously, "think I'll get some rest." The computer terminal chimed softly, and the control lights flicked methodically to black. The rabbit reached behind the main screen and took out a personal datapad, checked to make sure that the remote access link was off, then held it up to his face. After a few seconds, the pad made a few random-sounding beeps, and Perryman passed the pad over to Kovach.

"That," said the rabbit, "is what I saw."

Baptiste stood at the tiger's side, staring at something that made no sense whatsoever. Both pilots recognized the overall shape of the big white German shepherd on their team. Burned into the large biceps of his left arm was just what Perryman had described – a stylized, curving arrow with I8M, equally stylized, inside its description.

"And this is what makes it even more interesting."

The lop touched a control on the pad and the image changed – essentially the same, although now it looked almost like some sort of color negative. Baptiste asked, "This picture isn't light-based...?"

"Full spectrum, top to bottom. The Oculus has a lot of nice features like that. Makes night-vision a breeze." He pointed to the strange marking. "That is a radiation signature, not mere heat."

Kovach handed the pad back to him. "Erase that. And if you're smart, you'll erase it from your onboard chip too. You've got us as backup for your memory."

"Getting paranoid, tiger?"

"Getting practical. Don't leave any trails, and don't talk about it out in the open. Whatever this is, I think we can agree that someone didn't think that it was supposed to happen... and maybe it shouldn't have."

Perryman's natural eye narrowed somewhat. "Meaning?"

"Meaning we may have just stepped in something we weren't meant to know about."

The Husky sighed. "Just what I need: Drama and intrigue. What about Tolliver?"

"Not even sure he's out of sick bay yet." The rabbit shook his head. "If they knock him out, shave the fur down, do skin regeneration... there might not even be a scar to remember it by. I don't know what he may or may not have seen before they took him away; it's on a part of his arm that he might not have had a good look at."

"So which one of us gets to go pay a visit to our comrade in hospital?" The tiger looked at his companions in turn, their grins telling him what he had already suspected. Nodding, he said, "You realize Hazlitt thinks I'm trying to seduce him, right? If I keep visiting him so regularly..."

"Don't get caught, tiger," Baptiste punched him playfully in the arm. "Let us know what you find out."

"You'll both be here, I take it?" he teased.

"Not without a shower and some cabin freshener," the Husky waved her forepaw in front of her nose.

"Small price to pay," Kovach said to the lop. "I'd go for it."

"Out. Now." The rabbit grinned at the tiger. "And no towel for you."

"The story of my sad life." Kovach exited Perryman's cabin and made his way back again to sick bay. He kept is pace casual, even as his mind was racing, trying to grasp exactly what it was that had happened to them all. Usually good at multitasking, the pilot's mind was sufficiently engaged that he was only dimly aware of the brown-furred wolf with long black headfur who was following him.

6

The sick bay was quiet in what was the ship's late afternoon cycle. Kovach nodded to the nurse on duty, who smiled and nodded back. No restrictions, no appearance of guards or sentries on duty, no strong-arm stuff... after all the tiger had braced himself for, it was almost a disappointment. He padded silently through the entry section of the bay and into the miniature hospital ward. Another nurse, just coming out of the ward, nodded to him, his casually-worn off-duty uniform identifying him as one the Starhawk pilots. "He's in bed four, possibly napping. Just keep the noise down is all we ask."

Kovach mumbled his thanks, and the nurse left without another word. The ward was empty except for the Shepherd who, at first glance did indeed appear to be asleep. After he got closer, he saw the Shepherd's nose twitch. In an irritable voice, he grumbled, "What did you do, finally hump Perryman after all?"

The tiger grinned. "Not guilty. He was barred from the gym, so he worked up a sweat with his free weights in his cabin."

"Must have been important for you to have stayed there so long."

"The bunny can brew up a righteous funk."

Tolliver opened one eye slowly. "Glad he's feeling better." The clear golden eye held Kovach's for a moment, then looked left, right, and back again. The tiger shook his head minutely. "Never know what sort of devices they hook you up to in this place."

"Gotta fight for your rights in a hospital." Kovach put his paw gently over Tolliver's. Gazing directly into his eye, he used his fingers, index to little, in sequence, to squeeze a pattern onto the Shepherd's paw. All of the pilots had been trained in the technique. The covert communication couldn't convey a lot; its primary purpose was to establish, silently, a connection that would be difficult if not impossible for someone else to observe directly, let alone understand with any ease. The pattern asked for acknowledgement; Tolliver's head bobbed almost imperceptibly, his fingers squeezing firmly. The tiger's squeeze relayed caution. "How are you feeling?"

"Restless, if you want the truth." The Shepherd's fingers squeezed one of 16 two-digit patterns, this one indicating that he didn't think they were being watched. "Lot of fuss over a simple burn. Hurt like hell, but I've probably had worse over the years."

"I never did hear what caused it."

"Electrical, I think. I don't really remember much about it." Squeeze, index finger twice: *Lying.*

"I was told that there was some sort of program glitch, something that could indicate a possible security breech. Our pin drives have had the mission redacted, just as a precaution." Kovach's eyes said clearly what he thought of that explanation.

"Shame. I'd like to be able to remember better."

"Yeah, just to replay it, know what not to do next time. Guess it's all gone now." Squeeze: *Lying.*

"You and Perryman are okay, right?" the Shepherd asked.

"Yeah, no problems. Just told to take it easy all day. Get my strength back. Naturally, Perryman's got to exercise himself into a stupor. Nothing can keep that rabbit down. Can't hold a patch" *squeeze* "on him. Did you get to see what kind of scar you're gonna be left with?"

"Not a bit of it." Squeeze: *Lying.* "I'm told they did a first-rate dermal regen patch for me. May even be able to grow my fur back in the natural color instead of that scar-tissue white. I don't think anyone saw it." Squeeze, new pattern, index-little: *Verify?*

"I guess not." Squeeze: *Lying.* "When are they letting you out of here?"

"Probably tonight. Think they're just waiting to see if I'll need more pain meds, change the bandages for me before I go, all that stuff. I'd say I'd see you for a drink, but I'm figuring I'll probably need to stay off the stuff while I'm on pain meds."

"Good idea. Even synthahol has weird interactive effects. Make you see funny colors." Squeeze, little-little: *Will explain.*

The Shepherd chuckled softly, only partly as part of the show. "I might like to see that. But I'll be good." He looked down. "Hey, just because we're holding paws doesn't mean we're going steady or something, right?"

"Haven't even had our first kiss. Although I've been curious to find out if all those females are telling the truth about you."

"Only the ones who actually took out a measuring stick." Squeeze, new pattern, little-index: *Later contact.* "Thanks for coming by, Kovach."

"Always a pleasure to look after your tail."

"You would say that."

"Got a reputation to uphold." The tiger disengaged his paw, used it to pat Tolliver's uninjured shoulder. "Don't think this gets you out of future sims. We'll need you out there."

"Part of the team, tiger." The Shepherd's eyes conveyed meanings beyond his words. "See it through together."

Kovach clipped off a mock salute to Tolliver and left the ward.

As the tiger passed the front desk of the sick bay, he heard his named called. When he turned, he found a young orderly bearing a datapad and a slightly apologetic air. "I was about to have you paged, Lieutenant," he said. "Doc Hazlitt wanted to get one more set of readings on you, see how you're recovering from the accident."

"I feel fine."

The wolf, dressed in the white ship's uniform of a nurse or physician's assistant, actually seemed to blush. "I'm sure you're just fine, sir, but if I could ask you to…?" He waved in the direction of the examination beds. "It'll take about fifteen seconds for the scan, and we'll be done." He grinned. "You know the Doc when he doesn't get his way…"

Kovach chuckled. "Grounded for a week, no doubt. Talk about a bear with a sore paw… Yeah, sure, let's get it done."

The orderly indicated one of the beds. The pilot sat, then stretched out to ready himself for the scanner. The young male, all efficiency, pulled the privacy curtain on its tracks until they were entirely cut off from view of the rest of the sick bay. He turned to see the look on the tiger's face, and the wolf chuckled. "Sorry; habit."

"Here and I thought my reputation had preceded me."

"Actually, it has, but since you're technically my patient at the moment…"

The pilot, narrowly avoiding shifting himself into a more seductive pose, smiled with just enough suggestion to convey the right amount of lascivious humor. "I won't tell if you won't."

For a long moment, the orderly paused and seemed to consider the idea. He smiled ruefully at the tiger, finally saying, "You're just short of a temptation that I can't resist. If I didn't have my duty to consider…"

Kovach nodded. "I'll count that as a point in your favor. Congratulations, you've just made yourself that much more attractive. Let's talk again when duty isn't calling, eh?"

"Yes," the young brown-furred wolf said softly, almost sadly. "We'll talk again. I promise." He reached to his side, saying, "Here, let me put the monitor on. Just relax. This won't take long at all."

Rearranging his body a bit on the examination table (it was always best to be as comfortable as possible for these tests; helped make the readings look that much more calm and healthy), the tiger smiled, closed his eyes, and felt the sensor cuff placed almost tenderly around his left wrist. In the next instant, he was aware that his eyes could not open, his smile could not shift, and his body could not move.

"The effect is temporary, I swear it." The voice of the wolf was hot, soft, urgent in his ear. "Your autonomic functions are all working – you're still breathing normally, your heart is working, and your brain is working. Can you feel that? I don't want it this way, but it's the only way I can contact you." A paw touched his chest softly, then under his chin as if to verify the pulse. "Push way the fear and panic. I promise this will go on for only a very little time. You must listen to me closely."

The tiger heard a deep breath, wishing that he could take one himself, although he was indeed still breathing normally.

"You are not crazy. You've been hijacked, and that's not something I can explain right now. The simulation was hacked. I know – I'm the one who did it. Sorry for the scare, but I had to see if I was right. You're in danger, and so are a great many others.

I can't explain it all now, because you're Kovach now, and I need you to be you. Listen very closely: Kovach, Delta-Echo-Bravo niner seven niner Omega."

He knows my pilot designation code. But he could find…

"Override: You Are Number Six."

Despite being unable to move, Kovach felt something happening to him, something like a rippling effect from tip to toe, something changing, something not liking being changed, something that in other circumstances might actually cause pain, quite a lot of pain…

"Lock this in: Gemini. Schizoid Man equals Gemini."

The tiger still couldn't move, could not open his eyes, could not change the grin on his muzzle, and he knew that if he didn't scream soon, he would completely lose his mind.

He felt a tender kiss on his forehead. "Good luck, tiger. Go now."

Kovach's breathing and pulse began to quicken.

"Go. Wake up."

The tiger trembled, the shudder becoming more pronounced.

"Wake up."

A spasmodic jerking, some feeling of being able to move his limbs.

"Night, *wake up!*"

With a sharp cry, the tiger sat bolt upright in the large, comfortable bed, arms flailing until someone grabbed him (the wolf?), held his arms, called out to him.

"Night! It's okay! You're all right!"

Night? Trembling violently, breath heaving, the tiger stared pop-eyed into the darkness of the hotel room. His body stopped abruptly, and the ripple began again, the ripple, he had felt this before, from tip to toe, all the way down his body, like being put through some kind of wringer, being squeezed back into a tube, squirted through...

"Night?"

The tiger made himself stop, felt the arms that held him wrap themselves around him, felt himself pressed against the warm body of a (wolf) hyena, his hyena, his lover, Donovan, holding him, asking after him, saying his name... *his name...*

Gasping air like a drowning cat, Night grabbed Donovan bodily, pulled him into his arms, whimpered like he'd not done since he was a mewling kit. "What..." he managed slowly, "what happened?"

"Nightmare, I'm guessing. Bad one. Do you remember anything about it? What got you so scared?"

Trying to recover his breathing, the tiger searched his mind for clues, images, faces, anything. Nothing seemed to be there for him to find. There was nothing there. Only himself, his life, his simple and largely ordinary life.

He pulled away from Donovan a little and looked the hyena deeply in his eyes. "Hold me," he said. "Keep me safe."

"Won't let you go, love. Never let you go."

Night collapsed back on the bed, with Donovan curling protectively around him. He felt himself sweating, stinking of raw fear, his muscles aching as if they had been used and abused for some purpose he wasn't really built for. Too much volleyball, maybe. He should take it easier. This was a vacation after all, away from the project, away from the company, away from everything. It was bad enough having to spend so much time in sick bay, in hospital, in that damned bed, hooked up to every machine he never wanted to know about. He just wanted to rest. Just rest.

He felt warm breath in his ear. "You're okay, luv. I'll see to it. I'll never let you go. Just stay with me, Night. Stay with me, my tiger."

The hyena licked his ear and cheek tenderly, knowing exactly how to distract the tiger's worried mind. The world settled into its normalcy, the sound of the ocean along with the sea breeze coming in through the open window, the stirring of Donovan's soft, desirous grunting in his ear, the touching of his firm and sensual paws, making everything peaceful and safe again. They would hold each other, and kiss and caress and press together, turning the night into an impassioned expression of their love. They would collapse into each other's arms, breath chasing heated breath, whispering affectionate words to each other, and slowly falling asleep, quiet and safe.

By morning, the tiger would feel like his old self again.

7

The hot water both soothed and invigorated the tiger's muscles as he stood for a long time beneath the stinging spray. He luxuriated even as he realized that someone in this resort might have had a wicked sense of humor. The tiles, shower curtains, and various accents of the bathroom were indeed golden in color. To a degree, so were patches of Donovan's tawny fur (not through any external "applications"), although at the moment, he was still dozing quietly in bed while Night cleaned himself from nose to tail to get the disturbing scent of terror off of himself.

Truth told, he nearly had an unintentional exploration into watersports last night – he was within an ace of pissing himself, and he had no idea why. He tried to recall what had happened in that span of time just before he woke up feeling so terrified. No part of any dream came to mind, beyond a sensation of being unable to move, of a creepy sensation of having someone else in his head. There was nothing too weird about that. Night had read about a concept called the bicameral mind, which posited that the two lobes of the brain had the capability of creating that sensation. Some people called it God, when it might actually be nothing more than half of the brain trying to get the attention of the rest of itself. Self-induced schizophrenia, so to speak.

Night shook his head. That kind of science was beyond him, or so he told himself. He was much more comfortable crunching data, chewing programming statements, and otherwise making microprocessors dance to his tune. If that guy in the computer "grid" actually existed, Night would have made him his bitch, and then programmed him to like it. He smiled at the idea and gave himself a final once-over with the soap that the hotel had provided (lime, vetiver, and ginger, or so the wrapper had said – great combination, he might have to find out how to order bars of it for himself, since stealing soap from the hotel is, let's face it, just plain tacky). Finally satisfied that he smelled good enough to be allowed out in polite company, Night shut off the water, stepped out of the shower and began toweling himself.

The bathroom was huge, compared to the one in his own flat. He wasn't quite sure just why someone would need so much space in a bathroom, but it did contribute to the feel of luxury and relaxation – a big, open, new space that had no connections to anything from home beyond basic function. Even that could be questioned, to a degree; he had no bidet in his home, and he wasn't sure if he really wanted to experiment with this one. Great idea; mildly strange application.

He rubbed the towel vigorously through his long, dark brown headfur and looked at himself in the mirror. He supposed that vanity was a feline trait, from the rat-catchers to the regal. The tiger had ample reason to be more than a little vain, although he did try to exercise the occasional bit of modesty, if only just to keep in practice. His colors and stripes were vibrant, well-defined, and he kept his muscles buffed for any number of reasons (many of them related to his enjoyment of sex). As he looked at his face, his gaze was drawn to the twin vertical scar that bore witness to the near loss of his right eye, some years ago. His right ear, too, had a chunk missing from its otherwise perfect curvature, as if someone had taken a bite from it. Truth told, that's exactly what had happened. He remembered all too well what had brought that about, and like the philosopher's ring, it sobered him when he felt a desire to get cocky about his life.

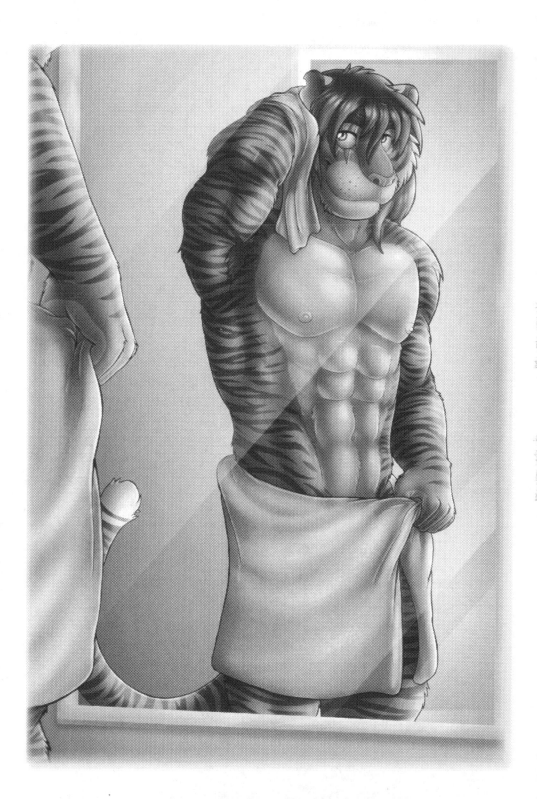

Night exited the bathroom and padded softly into the bedroom of the cabana. As he expected, Donovan was still asleep, his maw slightly open, making only the softest snoring noises, closer to a ragged purr than anything else. Night smiled with genuine affection. The hyena was becoming more and more a part of his life, and the tiger realized that he really didn't mind all that much. Was that love, he wondered, or merely pleasant complacency? He shook his head, not sure that he was ready to think about such conundrums just yet. He was hungry, and one of the great benefits of this resort was that meals were prepaid and always available, in either buffet or sit-down style. It was rather like being onboard a pleasure cruise ship, without the accompanying inconveniences of *mal de mer*, not to mention 90-foot tidal waves, icebergs, or other cinematic disasters.

The tiger dressed quickly and silently, leaving a note for Donovan to call him when he arose from his doze. He gathered wallet, room key, cell, and his ultrathin laptop, and set out for the main restaurant, determined to eat his weight in crepes, Eggs Benedict, oatmeal, link sausage, bacon (Canadian and any other form or nationality), cheese blintzes, and fruit cup. Swimming would have to wait.

* * * * *

At his table, where remnants of a savage culinary battle lay scattered across the tablecloth (in true Adam Richman style, it was Tiger Vs. Food, and Tiger won), Night perched his laptop in the space it was named for and checked his email. The wi-fi connectivity at the resort was powerful and wide of bandwidth, almost as good as a single dedicated hardwired connection. The tiger added this to the growing list of things the liked about the place. His email downloaded quickly and, from what his laptop's sniffers were telling him, securely. A few from well-wishing friends from home, several from various websites that he was beginning slowly to become bored with (another hint that his roaming days were coming to an end?), and one that would surely garner nasty looks from Donovan had he seen it – something from Waveforce.

Night wasn't about to let Donovan know that he was still working, just a little bit. The tiger didn't know what the big deal was. He'd been picked up by recruiters for Waveforce almost the moment he'd gotten his diploma in paw. The past several years were good ones, both for salary and advancement, and even more importantly, they were for the most part enjoyable. Few people get to do what they really love doing for a living, fewer still were particularly good at it. Night was fortunate in many ways. He had the ability both to conceive and design interactive gaming simulations at multiple levels, including being able to create self-correcting, heuristically advancing scenario-building technology that was going to take the MMORPG gaming experience to a whole new level. To make the pun, it was a real game-changer.

The tiger opened the email:

FROM: sbusby@waveforcebt.com
TO: noconnell@waveforcebt.com.
SUBJECT: Kabura-Ya Project

Night – per your inquiry, no data available; sources redacted. I'm sure all necessary data has been retained. The project can wait for your return. Get some sun, surf, and rest. You'll need your strength for when you get back. By the way, the small plant in your office was looking a little tired; I'll take it home to my greenhouse for the time you're gone. We could all use a little rest.

Sodus

A strange tingling at the back of Night's neck made itself known by making his fur shift quickly, as if reacting to a chill, or the sense of a threat. When it came to plants, his paws had ten black thumbs; he'd never kept a plant in his life, particularly not in his office. The tiger knew Sodus well enough to know that his getting cagy indicated one helluva level of paranoia. Sodus Busby was a jowly old mastiff who was probably the best project coordinator Night had ever worked with. Sodus knew the difference between riding herd over his programmers and riding their asses. He was good at keeping the company directors and big-wigs out of his team's collective headfur, as well as keeping his team working smoothly enough to keep the bean-counters happy. If the email meant what Night thought it meant, Sodus was telling him to take the conversation out of the company systems.

The tiger's fingers were a blur as he entered a series of commands and requests that created a tunnel VPN into his own home server. Securely connected, he first issued test parameters to ensure that his systems had not been interfered with; the results came back negative. Now protected by his Virtual Private Network, Night tapped out a quick response to Sodus' home email account:

Message received. My servers untouched as of now. What the hell is going on? Pawn's gambit.

He verified that he wanted to use that code key, sent the message and wondered how long it would be before Sodus could respond. Until then, he reasoned, there wasn't much he could do about it, other than keep Donovan from finding out that he was still at least a little bit the company's tiger. He took a few moments to verify that the home servers were up to date in all security areas, then closed the tunnel and turned off his laptop.

Sighing, tail twitching in an irritated swirl that the waiter misinterpreted as a complaint about the service, the tiger assured the young stoat in the crisply-starched livery that all was indeed well, just a few issues back home. Bowing slightly, the gently obsequious mustelid suggested that a relaxing hot stone massage might help set things right, and provided directions to the spa area, offering to alert the staff there of the tiger's impending arrival. Night smiled his thanks, tipped the young fur, and made his way toward what sounded like a great idea.

* * * * *

Swimming wasn't the only thing that would have to wait a little. The concierge at the spa was indeed expecting him, and he explained that it's not wise to have a massage too soon after eating, suggesting that Night might have a leisurely walk along the beach for perhaps half an hour, and then return. Leaving his laptop with the concierge, Night followed the pleasant orders, returning in time for his appointment. Leaving his clothes in the male's changing room, towel about his lean waist, he found the door with the "9" on it and knocked softly.

"Yes?" came a softly modulated male voice.

"I've an appointment for a massage? My name is Night."

"Yes, of course, do come in."

Opening the door, the tiger noticed that the metal number loosened and pivoted on its bottom nail. He looked in and said, "I'm sorry, I seem to have knocked your ornament loose."

"No worries," the young male chuckled. "It does that all the time. Come on in; you're expected."

Night's eyes adjusted quickly to the candle-filled darkness. His ears picked up on some very quiet, soothing music of the sort sometimes called "ambient." In the middle of the room, a sturdy and professionally designed massage table awaited, offering an optional padded loop for cradling the head, adjustable to suit just about any species. Various other add-ons would allow for longer or shorter arms and legs, an additional set of extensions that could accommodate some form of 'taur (despite or because of their rarity, many 'taurs could all the easier afford a luxury vacation like this one), and even some equipment that looked capable of handling wings, whether of the avian or saurian variety. The interior of the room large, open for movement, the walls done in dark paneling, hung with tapestries and cloth in muted tones, tranquil, restful, sound-dampening and soothing. The tiger felt himself relaxing already.

"Would you like to lie down? I'll get the stones ready. Have you had a hot stone massage before?"

"No, I haven't." He hesitated. "I'm not sure about etiquette," he smiled.

"Towels are optional," the young male said with a grin, turning to check some sort of warming machine. "I'm a professional masseur, not any other kind. I'm afraid your 'happy ending' will be the relaxation that you gain from the massage." He eyed Night briefly. "Off duty, I might be amenable to sharing a drink."

"I'll keep that in mind." The tiger doffed his towel and hung it over his arm, figuring he might offer at least a touch of modesty by letting it cover his backside. He reached out a forepaw to his host. "I'm Night."

The masseur turned to face him. The young brown-furred wolf smiled softly, his shoulder-length black headfur tossed back casually, his eyes bright and golden and knowing. He took the tiger's paw firmly in his own and shook it properly. "Good to meet you, Night. I'm called Gemini."

8

Night arranged himself face down on the table as Gemini helped him adjust the towel across his well-formed rump. "Let's make you comfortable. Would you like to use the ring? You can also rest your forearms on the low slats at each side, if you wish."

The tiger settled his head onto his forepaws, more the way he was used to sleeping. It also arched his back upward to be more available to the masseur. "Seems like they thought of everything."

"They, who?" the wolf asked, putting away the padded ring.

"Whoever designed these tables. Engineers aren't always so thorough."

"You speak from experience?"

"Guilty – but only in computer programs."

"Interesting field. Not that I know much about it." The voice paused, then asked, "Do you have any skin allergies, scent allergies, or any smells that you don't like?"

"I'm tempted to ask if you know the campfire scene in *Blazing Saddles*." Night heard a snort of laughter. "Sorry; I'm not very helpful, and I no doubt lack couth."

"Points for comedy, though." The masseur gently gathered Night's long, dark brown headfur and moved it carefully to the side, exposing his back entirely.

"No allergies that I know of. As for scents, I like the soaps that the hotel provides, if that's any help."

"Perfect. I think I know what lotion you'd like." A sound of liquid shaking in a bottle. "This stuff rinses out of fur wonderfully, don't worry. It'll help me to rub your muscles without pulling the fur. Two more questions: How firm should I be in rubbing your muscles, and how warm would you like the stones to be? Some folks get to 'Geez, that's hot!' faster than others."

The tiger hummed in consideration for a moment. "Start the massage about medium, and if you find something that needs some extra work, we'll go from there. I take it that you're not warming the stones up to lava-like temps?"

"Not even close," the wolf's voice laughed. "We'll test that too, when the time comes."

The sound of liquid squirting from a bottle, then paws rubbing together briskly. Night sighed deeply as he felt two strong wolf paws begin massaging his shoulders, near the neck. "Oh yeah," he breathed, letting his eyes close. "I'll try to keep my tail from whipping you out of sheer enjoyment."

"I'm sure I'll live. I have to laugh, though; I've barely started."

"Anticipation. I'm easily seduced by the promise of a great back rub. And you have strong forepaws. Lovely start."

"Goes with the job." A pause. "If you'll forgive me being a little personal, you have incredible musculature. You must work out a lot. Professional athlete?"

Night chuckled. "Desk jockey with a gym membership. Yeah, I'll admit to a little vanity too. No stereotyping about being feline."

"Wouldn't go there on a bet." The tiger felt the wolf's paws move expertly down his back, could almost see the masseur tilt his head to ask the question. "What sort of desk work? You mentioned programming…"

"Developmental stuff. Game design, mostly."

"Oooh, interesting! I love game theory and design. Not quite bright enough to do it for myself. You work with one of the big ones? ShellShock, Circle Phoenix, BioFare?"

"I smell a hardcore gamer."

"Not everyone's favorite perfume, I admit, especially after a weekend binge on *Lizard-Flight III: The Questioning.*"

The tiger grunted, partly in response to the excellent massage to his lower back, partly at the recognition of one of the competition's better efforts, despite the stupid title. "Waveforce."

"Waveforce Biosystems Technology?" The wolf whistled appreciatively. "Cutting edge bunch. Do I get to hear about what's on the drawing board, or is that too nosy?"

"Loose lips sink ships," Night chuckled, "as it says on one of the posters in my office. I don't think it's one of the World War Two originals, but the paranoia works the same."

"I can guess." The masseur stopped rubbing; sounds from behind weren't familiar, but neither were they mysterious. "Let me get one of the stones from the warmer. Stretch out a forepaw; I'll place one on there to test the temperature."

The tiger lifted his eyelids enough to see the wolf come around to the front of the table (a pleasant view all by itself), then more of the brown-furred wolf as he crouched slowly on his haunches and carefully put a stone into Night's paw. "Nice," the tiger murred.

"Not too hot?"

"Oh, very hot. But the stone is just the right temp."

"Flirt," the wolf's voice matched the smile on his muzzle. He stood up, taking the stone back, and Night felt the smooth, flat yet rounded stone being pushed at a snail's pace down his spine. The pressure and the heat seemed to melt his spinal column into complete relaxation. He breathed slowly, deeply, his eyes drooping closed again. The wolf left the stone, still hot and just a little heavy, at the base of the tiger's tail, and another stone moved slowly down the spine, eventually stopping a little distance from the first. After five stones had been placed, from base to tip, the masseur enquired, "Would you like me to tend to your legs and hind paws as well?"

"Yes, please do." Night noticed a note in his voice that could almost be considered begging. This guy knew what he was doing! "I hope you won't be shocked if I start purring."

"I'll consider it a particularly nice tip," the wolf's voice grinned. "So… not going to tell me any corporate secrets, eh?"

"Not even if you continue this horrid torture for another three hours," the tiger chuckled. "I'll never tell."

"We want… information," the masseur intoned ominously.

"You won't get it!"

"By hook or by crook, we will."

Night laughed. "One of my all-time favorite shows. Glad to know someone else enjoys it too. Who was your favorite Number Two?"

"All of them were good, but I still love Leo McKern."

"Good choice. Oooh… mmm…" The tiger's vocabulary was significantly impeded by the attentions that the wolf was giving to his hind paws. He was reduced to a singularly deep purring for several seconds before he regained his speaking voice. "Got a favorite episode?"

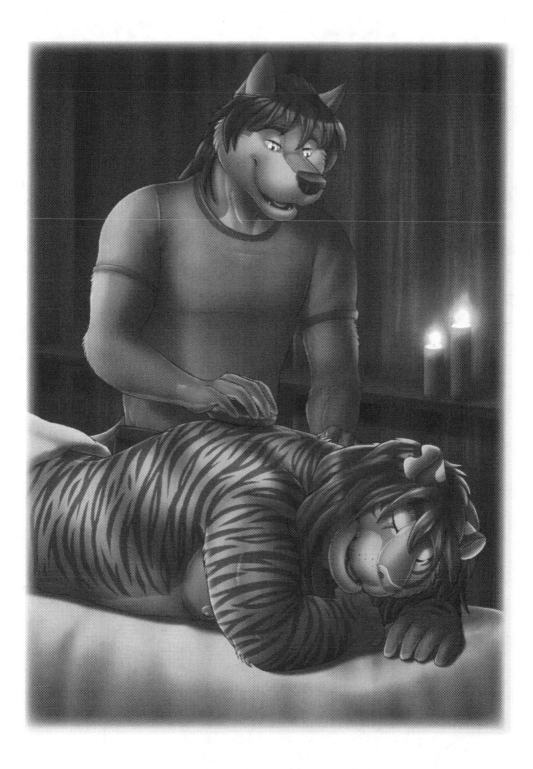

"You first."

"The Girl Who Was Death. It was the one episode of *The Prisoner* that was almost a comedy. Your turn."

"The Schizoid Man."

Night felt the fur across his entire body flicker, as if by a static charge. "Why that one?"

"Matches my name. Remember? I'm called Gemini."

Night tried to push himself off of the table, but in a moment he felt the weight of the wolf's entire body on top of him, holding him down. "What—?"

"Shh," hushed the wolf in his ear. "Stay calm. Use your mind. We've met before, haven't we?"

The tiger struggled harder, felt his arms pinned under his head and chest, felt the wolf's legs over his thighs and tucked under the table, giving the feline no purchase.

"You won't yell for help," the wolf said confidently. "You know I'm trying to help you."

"Help me do what?!"

"Remember. You've got to remember, Night. You've got to remember who you are... and who else you are."

"What do you mean?"

"Stay with me, Night. Keep your mind focused on yourself, on me, on my voice. Keep your mind focused on the here and now, and while you're doing that, try to think about the game. Think about the simulation. The one you created for Waveforce. Think about the simulation, Night, and try to remember the characters you created."

"How do you know about..." Night's body shuddered violently, quivering like a struck bell, shaking, convulsing, rippling...

"NO!" the wolf shouted. "Night, stay with me, stay... You are Number..."

"Six."

Night shook his head. The voice was crackling, as if through a speaker. "What..."

"Medusa Six, sound off."

The tiger's eyes snapped open. Screens, readouts, control panels. His body trembled violently, his brain ached with the effort of trying to stay focused, the smell of ginger, lime, and vetiver, the sound of weapons fire, hot stones upon his back, fire coursing through his mind...

One scream, long and loud enough to be heard outside of the simulation rooms and into the outer deck, and Lieutenant Kovach passed out.

9

Whispering.

Kovach came awake slowly, yet some sharp presence of mind told him to stay still, not give any indication that he was awake yet. He tried to sense where he was. Lying on his back, hard surface, scents of metal, of re-filtered air, of antiseptics – examination bed in sickbay? A memory of shock and screaming came back to him, but it was isolated from anything else. What had happened? A sim-pod, he remembered being in the sim-pod, but why had he screamed?

A raised voice: *Not for much longer, he won't!*

Another: *Keep it down, doctor, or I'll have you relieved.*

As if you could!

As if I wouldn't. Now shut up and listen…

Kovach recognized Hazlitt's voice, but the other was unknown to him. He risked the merest slit of space between his eyelids, holding his head still at first. He could see the ceiling, some of the equipment in his peripheral vision – sick bay, no question. The tiger moved his eyes left and right as far as he could, found nothing and no one in close range, decided to take the risk. He raised his head a little. The privacy curtains had been drawn around him; the voices were coming from just beyond it. They had gone back to whispering, too low for him to hear with any clarity. He was debating trying to duck out of sick bay and hide somewhere (on a ship in space, yeah, right, how far can you run, genius?) when the doc's voice was raised.

"Nurse! Where do you think you're going?"

"Just a routine check, doctor." Male voice, one that Kovach thought he recognized.

"Make it fast, then get out of here."

"Yes, doctor."

As the curtains slid back noisily in their track, Kovach quickly put his head down, closed his eyes, and did his best to look like he was still unconscious. He suspected that he did a lousy job; most people do. The curtains slid back into place again, metal rollers against the metal track. In the easy breathing through his nose, Kovach tried to get a sniff of his visitor, made it as far as recognizing something canine in the underlying scent, then felt the muzzle barely an inch from his ear.

"You probably think I'm here to kill you, or worse," the voice whispered quickly. "I'm not going to paralyze you this time. I need you to trust me, and I need to trust you, so here's the chance. Open your eyes. If you think I'm the enemy, call out for Hazlitt. If not, let me talk to you."

The tiger tried to make a rational choice, had no information to go on. His nose had caught something else, a scent of soap, something that smelled just a bit like lime and ginger, and his gut told him to trust the voice. He opened his eyes to see the brown-furred wolf with shoulder-length black headfur, the one who had done something to him... sometime... something about...

Kovach's lips barely moved as he breathed a single word: "Gemini."

The wolf nodded quickly, leaned back down to talk into his ear. "Got to talk fast. They can't keep you here forever; when you're released, find a way back down to the mess as casually as you can. I'll send someone you can trust, and they'll take you to me. We have to act quickly; your life is at stake, you can't take—"

The curtains rattled open. Kovach shut his eyes.

"Well?" the doctor asked petulantly. "Is the kit okay or not? And what the hell are you leaning in so close? Lookin' for a date?"

"No, doctor," the wolf replied evenly. "I thought I saw the remains of a contusion behind his left ear, per your report. He's been going in and out of a doze, I think, probably still needs some sleep."

"Codswallop," huffed the old bear, "what he needs is to quit clogging up my sick bay."

The tiger managed a low moan and mumbled, "Quiet down, why dontcha? My head's killin' me."

"Oh my, signs of life," Hazlitt declared derisively. "This could be a major medical finding – a pilot who actually seems to be attaining sentience."

"I'll tell Baptiste you made a pass at me."

The doctor had no immediate retort for the threat, so he snorted. "Nurse, let this excuse for a healthy male regain himself for an hour or so, then send him to bed without supper."

(I'll send you to supper without bed.)

"For medical or disciplinary reasons?" the nurse asked, grinning.

"For charitable and compassionate reasons; the mess is featuring some kind of fearsome farrago made from a synthetic that hasn't a traceable pedigree." Hazlitt looked back to the tiger, raising an eyebrow. "I suggest you avoid it, unless you want to end up back here again."

"Wilco, doc." Kovach tossed off a weak salute. He'd known Doc Hazlitt ever since he came aboard the *Heartwielder* after all, which was… The tiger tried to let the smile freeze on his lips even as the fur on the back of his neck tried to wriggle away on its own power. The memory conflicted with something else, something about a resort, an unclear image of a masseur, one who had asked him about his work with… with…

The wolf clapped a paw on the tiger's shoulder, squeezing slightly as if in warning. "I'll take good care of him, doc." Warm golden eyes peered into Kovach's, the slight edge in them confirming the message they had passed between them earlier. "Not like we can get good pilots just anywhere."

"Yes," the doctor admitted with a certain unease in his voice. "Well, get him out of here soon enough; I've got my own beauty sleep to look after." The bear pointed directly at Kovach. "Any smart remarks on that, and I'll ground your tail for a month."

"Wouldn't go there on a bet," the pilot managed with a smile. "Thanks, Doc."

The bear took himself out of the examination area with a grunt, and after several moments, Kovach let out a soft sigh. Turning to the wolf, he let his knotted eyebrows do the talking for him. The nurse looked around, his ears pivoting carefully, listening for anything he could catch that sounded out of place. He moved to the curtain, shifted it slightly, and peeked through. After a moment, he let the curtain fall back into place and turned to face the tiger.

"Okay, let me take some readings, just to be sure." The wolf shook his head gently to indicate that he was only acting for someone still within hearing range. "If the machines agree that you're all right, maybe I can get you out of here quickly. And I say you should get some food, if you can; just avoid anything with the word 'goulash' attached to it."

"Good advice," Kovach commented. "I like to know what it is that I'm eating. Concealed things give me indigestion."

The nurse smiled wryly at the comment and nodded again. "Always good to deal with what you can recognize." The wolf's paw made a rolling motion. "Readings look good, Lieutenant. Doc's already dictated a Review of Systems from last time; no changes, although we'll make note of any symptoms as they might appear. Think you can sit up for me? I'll lend a paw."

"I'll take all the help I can get." With the nurse supplying support to his back, Kovach managed to sit up on the examination table, grunting with some effort. His head felt a little swimmy, and he reached a forepaw up to hold it for a moment. Coming back around front, the nurse looked concerned, but Kovach shook his head gently, and the pup backed off. "So far, so good," the tiger observed. "The dancing pink elephants in the purple tights are a nice touch."

"Not like sick bay has much of a special effects budget. Take your time; I'm in no hurry. You may still have a bit of dizziness." His muzzle next to the pilot's ear, the nurse whispered, "Mess hall; I'll send someone. Please be careful."

Kovach nodded, speaking in a normal tone of voice. "They'll have to create a whole new diagnosis, eh? Kovach's Simulation Sickness. Just the way I want to be remembered." Positioning his muzzle to the nurse's ear, he whispered, "Harmony."

The wolf pulled back a little, his brows furrowed, looking confused. Kovach used his forepaw to make a movement like firing an old-fashioned six-shooter, and an idea locked into place for the nurse, who nodded and continued the show for the unseen listener. "They only name it after you if you die from it, and it sounds like the food will get you first. Up on your hind paws, flyboy."

Just before Kovach slid off the exam table and onto his hind paws, the wolf leaned in and kissed his muzzle gently. Pulling back, he looked at the tiger with a tender affection and mouthed the words, "For luck." Kovach snorted and grinned slightly – yet more movie references. Without too much effort, he managed to stand without falling over. "Well, gravity hasn't claimed another victim just yet," he remarked.

"You're doing fine. Try taking a step or two. Everything all right? We do have canes for use."

"On what, my backside? Kinky."

The wolf laughed. "Sorry, not the sort of service we provide at the sick bay."

"I'll keep that in mind." Kovach eyed the nurse briefly, and their mutual nods of the head told him that it was time to go. "I think I can make it to wherever I need to go. Thanks for your help."

"Anytime. If any symptoms return, come back or send a com-page for help."

"You'll come when called?" the tiger grinned. "Rather cliché canine trait."

The nurse actually blushed, which Kovach considered both sweet and perhaps a further sign that the wolf could be trusted. "I think that's called a straight line."

"Not from me. Thanks again." Before he left, the tiger mouthed the word *Gemini*. The wolf nodded slowly, and Kovach turned, opened the curtain, and left sick bay without incident. He needed answers. Conveniently enough, he also needed food, so he headed to the mess and hoped he'd find what he needed there. And since his mind needed something to chew on as much as his fangs, he wondered why he kept thinking about the ocean, and a resort, and a television program that was long before his time…

10

The plate sitting on the table in front of Kovach was picked clean. He had passed up the goulash (on medical advice) and taken very recognizable ingredients for a sandwich, some equally recognizable side dishes, and a large butterscotch-chip brownie that met with full approval from both his nose and tongue. His only risk was something called kirrinberry juice, which turned out to be pretty good, if a little tart. He'd had water to go along with it, just in case, and as he sipped on the last of it, he realized that he had no reason to linger. If he wanted to remain unsuspicious, he'd probably better leave soon… except that he was supposed to meet someone here, and he didn't think that he could risk going back to sick bay to find the nurse again.

Gemini.

Why did he know the wolf by that name? Worse still was the phrase that kept bouncing in his mind, *Schizoid Man equals Gemini*. The reference was unmistakable, but who beside himself was such a fan of the old British series? Sure, the Sarge knew some of the ancient Monty Python stuff, but who else knew about *The Prisoner*?

"Who let you out of the box, Kovach?"

Speaking of the bulldog… "Hey, Sarge. They had to let me go – lack of evidence."

"Lack of intelligence more like," Sumner growled low in his throat. He pulled up a chair, swung it around backwards, and folded his forearms on the back of it, giving the tiger a look so serious that he didn't even have a cigar in his mouth. He looked almost lost without it. "Tell me what happened."

"You're not going to like this, but it's the absolute truth: I don't know what happened." Kovach touched the bright orange pin drive on the lanyard around his neck. "Anything on these?"

The Sarge shook his large head. "They hardly had anything to redact. You went off just about the time that you were called on in the pre-launch systems check. That's part of what I was worried about – I had no idea what set you off. And you don't remember?"

"Sorry, boss." The tiger glanced casually around the largely empty mess, then back to the Sarge. "Don't mean to disrupt the drills."

"I admit, I prefer living in harmony."

Kovach froze to the spot, his eyebrows flicking minutely to ask the question. The Sarge's eyes held the tiger's, and his head dipped about a millimeter.

"You about ready to leave?" The bulldog asked.

"I was of two minds."

"Smart ass," the Sarge growled almost too low to hear.

"Yeah, I could use a walk."

Sumner stood up. "Got an interesting little dive you might like. No alcohol for you, but the atmosphere is nice."

"Lead the way."

* * * * *

The Sarge kept up a reasonably banal patter as they took a leisurely time getting to a destination that, if Kovach's reckoning were accurate, should have taken half the time to get to. It was clear that the Sarge didn't want to be followed. Upon arriving, the pilot wondered idly why he'd never even heard of the place before. It looked to be respectable, if understated and very slightly paws-off in its feel; if you weren't already a regular, or entering with a regular, subtle clues made it uncomfortable enough to send off the casual clientele. Upon entering, the Sarge offered a silent nod to a large Shepherd that could have been Tolliver's even bigger brother. The pup was apparently the joint's bouncer. He gave Sumner a nod in return and jerked his chin toward the back of the place. The bulldog led Kovach through the main bar and into a dark, quiet corner booth with a round table, high walls, and a certain now-familiar brown-furred wolf with enough presence of mind to look apologetic when Sumner and the tiger slid into place around the table.

"No drinks?" the Sarge grumped.

"Didn't know what you might want."

Through clenched teeth, Kovach rumbled, "How about a double-shot of 150-proof What the Crap Is This All About, with a No-Really chaser?"

For a long moment, the wolf simply sat, breathing slowly. The pilot wasn't sure if the nurse didn't really know anything after all, or if he couldn't make up his mind where to start. "I know how dumb this sounds," he began, "but how are you feeling?"

Kovach looked at him with a long, silent, sarcastic glare.

"Fair enough. Let me rephrase that. Are you feeling all in one piece? Do you feel anything out of place? Or at the risk of really opening the proverbial can of worms, are you who you think you are?"

"What the bloody hell have you gotten me into?" the tiger hissed angrily. "Is this a spy game or something?"

"That would be a 'something' category," the old bulldog said, "but I have no idea how to explain it to you."

"Neither do I," the wolf admitted. He glanced at Sumner, an unasked question in his eye.

"Can open, worms everywhere." He retrieved a cigar from a waist-pouch, jammed the end of it into the corner of his mouth, and set his jaw. "Let's do it."

"Do what?" Kovach asked, his muscles tense.

Quickly, the wolf spoke. "Kovach, Delta-Echo-Bravo niner seven niner Omega. Override: You are Number Six."

The tiger's gasp drew the brief attention of several nearby patrons who, knowing where they were and what sort of things happened here, went carefully back to their own business. In the booth, the wolf's forepaws went quickly to Kovach's own, one holding tightly, the other finding a pulse to help monitor the reaction.

"Tell me your name."

"Kovach." A pause. A frown. "O'Connell. Night O'Connell." The tiger shook his head hard. "What... who the hell..."

"Night," the wolf said clearly. "Hold on to your name, Night. Say it over and over if you have to. Hold on to your name and we can start filling in the rest."

Inside his mind, the tiger felt the absolute clashing of realities as two complete histories, two complete personalities, two complete versions of himself tried to assert themselves as the One True Self. "I can't..."

"Yes, Night, you can. Listen to me. The last memories that you had involved a hot stone massage at a tropical resort. Do you remember that? Do you remember me?"

Through the threatening tintinnabulation of the mother of all migraines, the tiger – Night – tried to focus on only one memory. A massage table, quiet music, candles, the strong paws of a good-looking young wolf massaging him, talking about work, talking about favorite television shows, talking about...

"...Gemini."

"Yes," the wolf said. "I introduced myself as Gemini. You remember."

"I think so." Night looked around himself, as if not recognizing his location. "Where are we? Is this that bar you were talking about?"

"No. It's quite different." Gemini breathed heavily. "Focus on you for a moment. What's your name again?"

"Night O'Connell."

"Are you employed?"

"Yes."

"Who by?"

"Waveforce Biosystems Technology."

"And what do you do for them?"

"Head Programmer." He forced a chuckle. "Always thought that was a good joke."

"How so?"

Night paused. "Classified stuff. Corporate intellectual copyright, that sort of thing."

"Okay, forget that for a while." Gemini flicked a glance at Sumner, who looked as if he'd wished he'd brought along a few extra cigars. "You were on vacation, right?"

The tiger made himself focus. "Yes."

"Any particular reason?"

"They made me take the time. I was working too hard." He paused, a slightly guilty look on his face. "Big project, took a lot of time."

"You really needed the time off, didn't you? In fact, you landed yourself in hospital."

Night waved a dismissive paw. "Just stress."

"Kabura-Ya."

The tiger stared. "How do you know that?"

Gemini reached into his pocket and withdrew a data pad. Using the stylus, he drew a curved arrow with what looked like I8M inside of it. "Have you seen that before?"

Lieutenant Kovach lurched forward, staring at the screen; Night had the sensation of not being in charge of his own body, of being pushed aside by someone who looked a lot like himself. Night knew that his head had moved closer to the data pad, that his eyes were seeing the symbol drawn there, but that it wasn't necessarily him who made is body move. The feeling was that someone else – another tiger, some kind of… pilot? – was answering instead of Night. "Tolliver's burn. That was the pattern of Tolliver's burn. Perryman's Oculus snapped an image of it before the medicos took Tolliver to sick bay."

"Someone's crashed the party, I see," Sarge mumbled.

The wolf spoke quickly. "Who are you? What's your name?"

"Kovach! You want the rank and serial number too?"

Gemini turned the pad around 180 degrees. "Have you seen that before?"

The pilot gasped, grunted, his physical body shaking as Night mentally pulled the other tiger backward and out of his way, so that he could stare at the shape before him – a curved arrow with the letters WBT inside it.

"Waveforce... the Kabura-Ya project."

The wolf smiled. "Welcome back, Night."

In some kind of stolen moment, in some non-existent space that (Night somehow knew) was inside his own mind, the programmer stared open-mawed at what appeared to be a duplicate of himself. The reflection-that-was-not-a-reflection stared back. There were differences, things that weren't necessarily important. The other tiger had no scar over is eye, no bite missing from his ear. His body seemed a little better formed, possibly even just a little younger, a sense of his being more physically trained than Night, of being someone who had gone through training (military?). There was something about his eyes that was different too, although maybe it was just Night's way of trying to enforce his own individuality, to insist that he was different, separate, *real*. Neither figured moved, seemingly suspended in a black void that existed as a staging area. Night had read stories about people with dissociative personality disorder, remembering the traumatic experience of effectively meeting someone else who was, actually, yourself. There was a place, those people had said, that was like a spotlight, a place where one personality could come forth to be dominant in the world. And now, there were two of him, there in the spotlight. Two. Of himself. In the spotlight.

For a long moment, the tiger breathed with slow, conscious effort. "He's still there," he whispered finally. "Like someone watching, wanting to take over. He wants to be in charge, because this is about his friends, and his work, and his life. He's the tough one, the one who's supposed to take care of himself. I don't think he trusts me. I'm not sure that I trust either of us..." Carefully, he raised his eyes to the wolf. "Am I crazy?"

"No more than any other genius." Gemini smiled softly. "To be more exact, you are Night O'Connell, brilliant programmer and visionary. Lieutenant Ambrose Bierce Kovach is a character that you created. He has a complete background, personal history, education records, family background, training experience, and most recently, the experiences aboard the *Heartwielder* as the pilot of a Starhawk class recon fighter vessel. You created him to be as complete a personal experience as possible, for whoever wanted to play his character inside the most expansive, total-immersion gaming experience ever created. The background was necessary to help the player have resources to call on for both mission and non-mission experiences. He isn't real, not in any corporeal sense.

"At least," the wolf said softly, "he wasn't."

11

"Are you saying this is a simulation?" Night looked first to Gemini, then Sumner, trying to get some idea of what the hell was going on. "I'm existing in some kind of game simulation?"

"This is where it gets complicated."

"No, surely not." The tiger felt his tail lashing under the table and tried to keep it still. "How could this possibly get complicated?"

The wolf sighed yet again. "I'll try to keep this in order, but I'm not sure how well I can do. Start with how you got hired at Waveforce in the first place. Right out of college, right?"

"More or less, yes." Night's brows knotted, finding himself running through his history, not quite reliving it. "They had the most interesting offer on the table, and I took it. Good money, good project, good company… seemed like something to ride on for a while."

"Tell me about the central concept of the Kabura-Ya project." Gemini raised a forestalling forepaw. "I know, corporate classified. Would you rather I told you about it?"

"What do you think you know?"

"The Kabura-Ya, in history, is the Japanese turnip-headed arrow, the whistling arrow. They were used as part of a ritual in feudal Japan before formal medieval battles. The name was chosen for this product partly for whimsy, partly for a description of the effect of the system itself. The idea was to find a way to create a game interface that allowed a player to 'jack-in' to the system without a direct hookup. In theory, anyone could find a way to implant what some sci-fi writers called 'wetware' directly into the brain or nervous system, but apart from costs and obvious inherent dangers, it's just not a good idea. The alternative was to find another way into the brain without needing a physical connection, and two basic ideas were examined. One was brainwave-sensing equipment, something like EEG connections on steroids, but the hardware wasn't quite advanced enough. The other method was through the eyes, using a combination of—"

"…low-wavelength laser input and biofeedback signals directly from the physical movement of the eyes." Night nodded. "Yeah, you've got the background. We used the symbol of the whistling arrow because when the system activates, it…" The tiger's eyes got very wide. "It triggers a kind of calibration through the body that alerts you to its presence, its function. You know that you're connected, because you feel the change… like a ripple though the body."

Gemini nodded. "It's the body's way of helping the input signals link in, so that the experience is like total immersion. Under ordinary circumstances, you can still hear and sense what's going on around your physical body. The thing was supposed to be a game, not a prison." The wolf cocked his head slightly. "Did you ever wonder where the technology came from?"

"Not that huge a breakthrough, in a way," the tiger demurred. "The theories have been around since the 1980s or so, thanks to films like Michael Crichton's *Looker*. I just figured someone – probably military, first – had figured out the tech, and I was brought in to help program the simulations to test them out."

"Why video games? As you said, why not military use?"

Night's muzzle curved up in a nasty, humorless grin. "I'm not entirely naïve. There's only one thing that would promote research at this level: Power. That power has to take the form of war or money. As long as I didn't have to look at the military applications of it, I was glad to think I'd be making a fortune by investing in the company that created a breakthrough game technology."

"And if the original technology wasn't there?"

"What are you saying?"

Sumner sat back in the booth looking tired, but his eyes were still sharp and interested. "Night. That's your name? Look, I don't know you. I've worked with Kovach, though. Can you let yourself relax enough to see what he sees?" The bulldog shook his head. "Maybe I'm not saying it right, but where we are now is where Kovach has been for the last several weeks or so. If you can know what he knows, and still keep yourself as who you are, it'll save some time." The cigar worked and shifted in his muzzle as he ground his teeth. "Hell, even I don't know what I just said."

"No, it's a good idea," Gemini nodded. "You created the original character. There's more to him now, because of the simulations, the experiences – *his* experiences. Can you sense that?"

Night still hoped that, deep down, he was simply insane, and that someone would come along soon with one of those tuxedo jackets that had wrap-around sleeves that hook into the back, and a nice cocktail of pills that would make everything all trees and flowers and chirping birds. In the meantime, he was stuck for a way to deal with all of this. "Okay," he said. "If I start spouting off like a refugee from a bad *Star Wars* rip-off, just shoot me."

The tiger closed his eyes, not having the faintest idea what to do, until he felt a gentle paw touch his shoulder, knowing that the sensation wasn't physically produced. He was back in that space that felt like a stage, with a single spotlight coming from somewhere high above, just out of sight. He turned (again, feeling the sensations without doing anything physical) to see the other tiger standing right in front of him – the tiger that was his height, size, shape, the tiger that essentially himself, yet different. The eyes stared back at him, eyes not used to betraying anything like fear yet hinting that maybe, just maybe, he was as scared as Night felt.

Am I real? Did you make me up? the other tiger said softly, like a voice in a dream.

I don't know, Night answered, not speaking.

I'm real. I have to be. I can feel my body, feel my heart…

Night finished the thought. *…or is it my heart?*

The pilot stood, wearing his uniform casually, rather than togged up for actual flight or battle. Night realized that he – his body, or maybe not his body, whatever was back at the bar – was wearing the same thing, a space fleet's version of BDUs. *Part of me is thinking this is some kind of psy-ops trick, or another training test. And part of me is thinking that I need to take control of myself. Of you. That you can't be real, that you're trying to steal me.*

Although not really in a physical space during this exchange, Night felt himself tremble. *Why don't you?*

Because… The pilot's brow furrowed slightly. *I'm you. Or part of you, or something. I don't know how I know that. I don't know if I'm supposed to know that. But somehow, I know that we have to work together to figure this out.*

Why?

Because I think we really are two people. I started out in your mind, but I do have a life. You have a life somewhere, making games. I have a life here, on this ship.

Ship?

Kovach reached a forepaw toward Night. *Let's see if this works. Take my paw.*

How can I do that? This is just thought, just… Hell, I don't know what it is.

I don't either. Go with it, let's see what happens.

Night reached out and touched the pilot, then inhaled sharply, his eyes – the physical eyes, the body's eyes, his body, Kovach's body – his eyes flying open. He felt Gemini put his paws to his shoulders and shake him gently.

"Night! Are you all right?"

"I'm…" The tiger gulped involuntarily, looking around him. "I'm on a spaceship?"

"The *Heartwielder*," Sumner said. "I'm wagering that wasn't part of your simulation scenario."

Remembering to breathe, Night shook his head. "Details I never put in. The game wasn't specific to a single ship, certainly not like this. Are we really…?"

"Yes." Gemini turned Night's head so that he could look him in the eyes. "This is not simulation, Night. That's what I'm trying to explain to you. This is physical, tangible reality. The planet you live on is a long way from here, and you – Night O'Connell – are still there. You're not in your own body. I know how crazy that sounds, but I'm serious. The term is 'hijacking;' it's dangerous, it's unethical, and it's something that we're trying to stop. We're trying to get you back to where you belong, and to make sure that Kovach's connection to you is severed so that you won't have this happen again."

The tiger stared, barely comprehending. "How…? Why…?"

"The technology is here," Sumner grumbled, "but the theoretical breakthroughs came from you. Your programming techniques actually make the technology work. I have no idea how they found you, but somehow they found your planet, and I guess from there, the rest was easy for them."

"Whoever put the plans into effect in your company came from here." The wolf kept his eyes on Night. "You worked up a program that included everything they needed, or almost everything. What they needed wasn't so much the ability for a total-immersion simulation system. They needed someone who could outthink such a system. Only someone who could program something as complex and detailed as the Kabura-Ya project – only you – could give them the raw intuition that they need to solve their problem."

"Which is?"

"The Bradbury Drive."

Night blinked, felt as if Kovach had put the information there in his mind to reference, and slowly nodded. "No one here knows how it works, do they?"

"It's a problem like your own," Sumner nodded. "We had technology, you had theoretical constructs for it. Someone else out there, as far as we can tell, has found some theoretical knowledge for their own technology, and we can't figure out how it works. We put the facts into the simulation, and someone – not me, I swear it – got you in here to see if you could figure out how it worked."

"Then the…" Night searched Kovach's memory for a moment. "…plasma shuriken? Is that real?"

"Yep," the Sarge nodded. "And you saw what happened in the simulation… or Kovach did."

"It triggered a recalibration," Night nodded. "The simulation itself overloaded, but somehow I was actually jacked into it." He considered further. "What about the other two?"

"That was my fault," Gemini admitted, blushing a little. "I hacked the Phibriglex-62 sim and created some feedback that... well, I wanted to distract them away from you, and away from testing the sim itself, at least for a while. Perryman and Tolliver were okay."

"You tried to send me a message," the tiger realized, his eyebrows rising. "The Kabura-Ya emblem... except that Kovach didn't know what it was."

"I think I was hoping that some part of you – Night – was close enough to the surface of Kovach's consciousness to recognize it, see it as a message. The division between the two of you is strong."

"Was," Night said softly. Somewhere inside himself, he felt something like gratitude from the other self that waited in his mind with a rough patience forged from sheer cussedness. He frowned. "Wait, let me understand something. This isn't a simulation, right? This is all real. This body is real. But... it's not mine?"

"The body belongs to Kovach, when it's actually occupied."

The tiger shuddered, feeling his counterpoint doing the same in spite of both of them. "Am I going to regret asking?"

Gemini grimaced. "You created the character of Lieutenant Ambrose Bierce Kovach. In order to make it easier for you to slip into this world, so that you could perform the simulation for them, they... created him. Some sort of cloning and memory imprinting, I don't begin to understand it."

"You mean I'm not really real?"

The wolf started. "Kovach?"

"It's okay; Night is here. He's letting me speak. We're sort of getting used to it or something. He's said something about 'sharing the spotlight,' whatever that means. Yes, I'm Kovach. Or at least I think I am. And what you're telling me is that I'm not real."

"No, you're real enough." Gemini tried to smile but didn't seem at all sure if he was doing it very well. "How you started may seem creepy, but you have to remember that you've had real, personal experiences for these past many weeks, maybe months. Those aren't programming or simulations – those are really you. That's your body. Night has his own, back on Earth somewhere, and we'll find a way to get you both back where you belong."

The tiger sighed deeply enough for two, then said, "What happens to our bodies when we're not in them?"

The wolf frowned again. "Who's talking?"

"Maybe both of us. Is that so difficult for Gemini to accept?"

"You have a point," Gemini actually managed to laugh. "I don't have all the answers. All I can say is that no one has found either of you comatose, uncommunicative, or otherwise out of it. I've never had that experience either, but my case is a little different."

The thought took a moment to form in Night's mind. "The masseur, on Earth…"

"He's my twin. My actual, physical twin." The wolf smiled. "I miss him like hell, but we have good communication through all this. Not quite as close as you and Kovach, perhaps, but close."

"You came from Earth?"

"No. One of the outer colonies. He went to Earth a while back. He found you first, put the idea together about what was happening, and then… we've been trying to puzzle this thing out for a long time. We still don't have all the answers."

Night sank back in the booth, hung his head back against the padded rest and sighed yet again. After a moment, he chuckled. "You know how I know this is real and not a simulation?"

"How?"

"I have to go piss. Never heard of a simulation programming in potty breaks. Where's the loo?"

As the tiger rose, Sumner got up as well. "Don't get any ideas, kitty," he grumbled. "I'm just covering your tail, not trying to grab it."

"Fair enough. We might need a guard after all."

The males' room wasn't overly large, but it was clean and well-kept. Night used the facilities readily enough, somehow managing to overcome the sensation of being pee-shy about someone actually inside his head having no choice but to watch what was going on. He finished the necessary task, then moved to the basin to wash his paws.

There's an old pilot's joke, Kovach spoke softly in his head. *A grunt and a pilot are in the males' room together, using the urinals. After they're done, the grunt stops at the basin to wash his paws and the pilot starts to leave. The grunt says, 'In the Corps, they taught us to wash our paws after using the toilet.' The pilot says, 'In flight school, they taught us not to piss on ourselves.'*

Night laughed, finished washing his paws. "Just habit with me," he said aloud, "although it's your body, so maybe I shouldn't take such liberties."

I'm just amused that you shake three times, like I do. I doubt you programmed that in.

"Details, details," Night said. "Just be glad..."

He stopped and looked closely in the mirror. The face that looked back at him was very much like his own, enough that he could easily have thought of it as his own. For the first time, he looked at the physical face to match the one he saw in his own mind. He reached up a forepaw and traced the space – the unscarred space – over his right eye, gently. Inside his mind, he felt as if Kovach were standing behind him, his forepaw on Night's shoulder, looking at the reflection in the mirror with tender sympathy.

I saw how that happened, Kovach's soft, slightly awed voice said. *I saw it in your memories. That must have hurt.*

"In more ways than one," Night whispered. Derek, his name was. He was the first male that Night had ever loved, the first he had ever dared to tell. The response from the older male was brutal, although only the damage to the eye and ear was visible now. Most of the other scars had healed – the physical ones, at least. He breathed deeply and shook off the memory. It was no good reliving it, for himself or for Kovach. There was too much to do now, too much at stake. He checked himself in the mirror once more, made sure everything was in place, clothing, lanyard, pin drive...

He frowned. He touched the bright orange pin drive. Night found himself accessing Kovach's memories, not like a computer finds data, but as a real person remembers after having forgotten something. Time condensed, as it does with that odd sensation of memory, where everything falls into place at the same instant, yet individual moments are more or less relived in real time. Night, or perhaps Kovach, was remembering facts about the pin, how its use was quotidian to a pilot, never without it, using it for everything, especially simulations and real flights as well. The pin was, in part, a data recorder, bright orange, the color chosen for the same reason that various flying and space vehicles had a "black box" which was also colored bright orange – easier to spot in wreckage, should it come to that. It was one of the earliest decisions, Kovach remembered, for the pilots of the Starhawk class ships…

(he took the red pin drive from his neck, to jack into the simulation…)

(he waved the blue pin drive at the register in the mess…)

Night looked at the reflection of Kovach in the mirror. "We're being played."

12

I don't understand. Kovach's voice was as real to Night as if the pilot were a physical being who had just spoken to him. *What to you mean, played?*

"Played, used, manipulated." Night looked at his reflection in the mirror, as if he thought he could see Kovach peering back at him through his eyes. "This isn't right. There are too many things out of place."

What do you—

"We need a quiet place to think, and to talk. As weird as that sounds." Night silently tapped some part of Kovach's history, feeling the peculiar sensation of learning something in just that moment that he had known for weeks, perhaps months – the assignment, shifting the gear into the new quarters, making the space his own, for whatever time he would be aboard. "Think we can make excuses and get to your cabin?"

Where it all started, the pilot said, as if seeing the idea in Night's own mind. *Yeah. They must know you're tired as hell after all this. Get them to take you home.*

Night nodded at himself and turned just as the Sarge opened the outer door. "You fall in?"

"Yeah," the tiger grinned at him, "and I had to swim my way through the slime in garbage compactor 3263827."

The bulldog snorted a laugh. "You and your movie references. C'mon, let's get you out of here."

"Good idea; I'm exhausted."

Back at the table, Night didn't even bother to sit down. He looked at the wolf and, although he wanted to yawn to add credence to his story, thought better of it. "This is a lot to take in," he said. "I doubt there's anything more we can do tonight. How about I go back to Kovach's quarters and sleep it off?"

Gemini nodded. "I'll take you back."

Night was about to object but felt the equivalent of Kovach's paw on his shoulder. "Good idea," Kovach spoke for him. "I don't know anything about this place."

"Isn't Kovach still...?"

Kovach continued the pretense, saying, "I think he's still a little disoriented. Probably we both are."

You ain't kiddin', Night thought.

The wolf looked at the Sarge. "I'll get him back. We'll be fine."

"Good. I got my reputation to think of." He grinned a little crookedly and went over to the bar where a full-figured but quite nice looking young vixen was seated. Whatever he said to her, it seemed to work, as both were grinning at each other, and the vixen's tail was flicking flirtatiously at the bulldog's legs.

"I guess I've got mine to think of," Kovach teased the young wolf. Night wasn't entirely sure that the pick-up line was a good idea, but Gemini seemed to appreciate it.

"I'm not on duty now, am I?" A slight blush appeared on the wolf's cheeks. "I think my twin offered to have a drink with you, and I..." The blush deepened. "I think I flirted with Kovach, whether I meant to or not. Do you two really look like each other, physically?"

Walking out of the bar, Kovach and Night paused, as each considered how to answer the question. "Pretty much, I think," Night answered, in his mind putting a paw to Kovach's shoulder. "Kovach must work out more than I do; he's got good muscles. I'm not entirely sure I'm used to them." *Thanks for the compliment, bro,* Kovach thought. "I'd hate to get caught up in a flight simulation, though; I wouldn't have his muscle memory."

Gemini nodded. "It's one thing that they had to work out when creating Kovach as a physical being. The whole idea of him being military was…" The wolf hesitated, looked up into the tiger's face. "I hope I'm not saying anything that will upset him. This is a whole new concept for me."

"For *you?*" Night said in disbelief. Then managed a smile for the embarrassed wolf's benefit. "It's almost like he's asleep, I think." *Just a cover, tiger.* Night felt Kovach nod. "Maybe he and I can have a conversation and figure out what to do. He needs his life, and I need mine. There's got to be some way to fix this."

Wolf and tiger walked through the various parts of the vast ship, a strange and futuristic variation of walking through city streets to get back Kovach's quarters. Night wasn't expected to know his way, and the wolf, unsure who might be listening, kept the minimal conversation light and banal. Kovach gently kept Night from getting too freaked out by seeing various bits of decking, hardware, cables, hoses, the paraphernalia of a space-faring craft that Night knew only from movies and television. On several occasions, Night thought that the place resembled a movie set, and catching the references and recollections from Night's memory, Kovach had to agree with him. He (Kovach) had lived in it for quite a while by this time, but he could easily see how certain seemingly endless stretches of the ship looked like any other. What disturbed Kovach was that Night seemed to find that idea suspicious.

Before too long, they arrived at a door that Kovach knew well. "Is this it?" Night asked, knowing he'd be expected not to recognize it.

"Yes." Gemini pointed to a metal plate with KOVACH, 1ST LT A B inscribed on it. The wolf hesitated again, blushing. "Shall I leave you alone?"

Night laughed. "That's a relative statement, isn't it?" He sobered, getting the gist of Kovach's feelings on the subject. "I'd like to invite you in – after all, both Kovach and I have reputations to keep up! – but it's a little… strange. If you and I were to… well, at this point, it wouldn't really be either Kovach or myself, would it?"

The wolf's blush deepened. "I hadn't thought of it like that. I'm sorry."

"Don't be; this is all new to me too." Night, with Kovach's approval, bent down to kiss the young wolf gently on his muzzle. "I think I can safely say that's from both of us."

Gemini's smile almost reached his ears. "Thank you." He shifted, coughed a little, finally took a step backward. "Okay. Yeah. I'll say good night then. Okay if I come get you for breakfast?"

"Probably a good idea. I may not know where to go." Night patted the wolf on his shoulder, smiled, and entered his cabin. "See you then."

"G'night… Night." He chuckled as the door closed.

Night looked around the cabin as best he could, but it was dark. Kovach touched his shoulder, and they said, "Lights, full." As the room illuminated, Night nodded and said, "Thanks. I sort of remember that."

Pardon my paranoia, Kovach said, without using Night's vocal cords, *but if we can do this without actually speaking, it might be a good idea. I have no idea who might be listening.*

Oh, they're listening, you can bet on it. They can't help but listen. We're the experiment.

Explain that.

Night recognized the kitchenette area, found the refrigerator, and happily found some milk in there. He took a drink from the bottle, then caught himself. *Sorry,* he thought, embarrassed.

If I'm based on you, then I know where I got that bachelor's habit from.

Not something I programmed into the character you're based on. That's part of my point. Night moved to the recliner and settled himself into it, amazed at the sensation of the chair being new (to him) and familiar (to Kovach). Keeping his muzzle shut except to sip at the milk, he started making his case. *You're too complete. I couldn't possibly program in this level of detail. It's like they took me, changed key details of history, and overlaid the fighter pilot components. Habits, like drinking milk out of the bottle, that's completely me.*

But I do it too.

Night sighed audibly, and in his mind he felt as if he had turned the other tiger to face him, to look into his eyes. *You know about the television program* The Prisoner, *right?*

Yes.

And Monty Python, and Star Wars, and all of that.

Loved 'em since I was a kitten.

So do I. And that's why I programmed in so many in-jokes into my scripts, to put humor into the program for the gamer nerds who liked the same things I do.

The mental image of Kovach seemed too wide-eyed, too knowing, as if he already suspected the answer. *Earth things,* he said. *Why would I know those?*

More than that: Why would Sarge know them? Night felt his heart pounding, as if sympathizing with Kovach's own fear. *I'm fascinated by things that happened in the several decades before I was born. I don't know if you'll know what I'm talking about here… In 1962, Earth came within an ace of destroying itself with nuclear weapons. The two great superpowers of the day, the US and the USSR, got into a deadly pissing match over who would have more influence over the presumably independent island of Cuba. Russia tried to sneak in nuclear weapons, which would have given them the ability to strike almost every city in the US. Part of the US response was to use a real, planned military exercise as the cover for getting ready for a confrontation that, at that time, the public did not know was about to happen. The code name for that exercise was Phibriglex-62.*

Like the simulation. Kovach, a mental image as real to Night as a physical being, reached out a trembling paw. Night took it, keeping his eyes on the tiger's face. *Sarge couldn't know that, unless…* The pilot looked directly into Night's eyes. *Is he like you? Like Gemini? Do you all have counterparts on Earth?*

Kovach… I need you to think about one more thing. The lanyard. The pin drive. What color is it?

Bright orange, the pilot answered without hesitation. *Almost fluorescent bright. Like flight recorders and such, so that…*

In that strange mindspace where they faced each other, Night gripped the pilot's shoulders, as the (other) tiger blinked in confusion. *The first simulation,* he whispered. *The first time you flew and found the ship with the Bradbury drive. The pin was red. And later, after sick bay, when you met … Baptiste, you met Baptiste in the mess, and the pin was blue. After each recalibration, the pin changed color.*

But it's always been… Kovach's ears splayed, his brows knitting together, his tail lashing, his voice near to being a whimper. *Night, I don't understand. You have to tell me. Tell me what it means.*

It's a program glitch. It's changing with each new iteration of the program, because it's trying to correct itself, improve itself.

Program?

Night nodded slowly. *Yes. I'm sorry, Kovach. This isn't real. It's a simulation.*

13

Night could feel, physically, the shudder that went through Kovach as the implications made themselves known. *No,* he said, but without any sense of conviction. *I'm real. I have to be. I've been on this ship for weeks, maybe months, too long for me to remember clearly. Even if you created the original 'me,' I've lived here, experienced things, learned things… I'm more than you created.*

Yes. Kovach's body still sat in the recliner, sipping milk, while the conversation went on inside his head. But even that, Night realized, was almost surely being monitored from somewhere. *All of this is more than I created. I was working on a simulation, yes, but it wasn't focused on board a ship like this. I didn't create that dive we were in a little while ago, I didn't create this cabin, or the characters you've been interacting with. Some of them were sketched out, yes, but not to any great degree. This has all been added to, grown, evolved.*

But not by you?

Not by me.

Then what the hell…? Kovach seemed to look at Night, as if the two of them were actually in a room together. *This is all in your head. I mean, you and I, we're both in your head. In this moment, we're in your head.*

That's about as good as it gets.

But what's outside your head, that's a simulation.

Night winced. *In theory, it's all in my head, meaning that the simulation is being caused by something – a computer system of some kind, and damned fancy for all that – but the things out there, including what I'm calling 'my body' or 'our body' at this point, is all a simulation. None of it is real. Only this consciousness. My consciousness.* He paused. *And you're a part of that, Kovach. You're part of me.*

But I'm not actually me.

The tiger felt himself looking at himself, at Kovach, realizing for the first time what a tin-plated copper-bottomed pitiful excuse for a god he was. He had created a character, and some damned machine somewhere had created life, or what passed for it. And the last thing he had time for was a philosophical debate.

Kovach, I haven't got all the answers. I only know that I have to get myself out of this simulation. Gemini used the term 'hijacked.' I don't know if I can trust him – for all we know, he's simulated also – but it makes sense in a way. Somehow, my consciousness has been thrown into this simulation directly. In this reality, Gemini has a 'twin brother' – perhaps a real person in my own world who is representing himself in this simulation as his own twin. He's somehow jacked into this simulation as well. Night felt himself shaking his head. *It's like a bad rip-off of* Tron, *but it gets the job done.*

I know that reference. You watched it, but I know… I remember… or whatever… Kovach looked at Night. *Then I'm like a program in that film.*

Maybe. And somehow, I've been hijacked, against my will, into this simulation.

Why?

They want something. Maybe just to observe how I react.

The pilot shook his head. *Got to be more than that.* His muzzle twisted into a wry smirk. *You seem to have made me more inquisitive than most.*

That goes with being feline, Night managed to grin. *Okay, let me hear your thinking. You know more about what's been going on here over the past few weeks; all that stuff that I didn't program, that's what gives you the edge here.*

For a moment, Kovach seemed only to stand there and breathe. Then, with a soft smile, he nodded. *Okay. Everything has been about the Phibriglex-62 sim. As far as I can tell, it was created because of the reports about the Bradbury Drive. Even Gemini said that he thought the drive was the reason they brought you here. The question is, did they bring you here to create it, or to counteract it?*

Tell me what you know about it, what's come through in the reports and other information. How did you hear about it? Briefings? News reports?

Confidential reports. So far as I know, the general public hasn't heard of a Bradbury Drive, at least no one who's not aboard the ship. There are looky-loos who watch the sim runs, but they have no idea what's real and what's… The pilot paused as if he just realized what he was saying. Night reached out to grip his shoulder, both of them knowing that it wasn't really a touch, yet it was somehow comforting anyway. Regaining himself a little, Kovach took up the thought again. *The idea is still considered to be a theory, no known prototype. That would seem to indicate that you're supposed to create it for them. The fact that we found it in the sim run… or sort of found it, anyway.*

Run through Phibriglex-62 in your head again. Take me with you. What started it?

Kovach found that he could recall every moment of the Snake Lady simulation run, this time with the sensation of having Night right there in the cockpit with him. The first ship was a creampuff offering to warm things up, and then Sarge landed them in the poo. Tolliver met the ship, which tried to run off; Perryman joined in to pincer the ship, which powered weapons, then backed down when they realized that the Starhawks had shurikens. The two pilots escorted the ship briefly, broke off when they were told to, and then Baptiste caught the radiation signature of a special type of drive engine.

Then everything went nuts. Rains tried to fly through the building warp bubble, or rather through the space where the bubble was forming, his wake disrupting the formation for a few seconds... wait a minute... Kovach moved his arms, his paws reaching for controls that weren't really there, but the motion helped him concentrate his memory, replaying it for Night's edification. *The theory behind the drive is a form of folding space, as literally as that phrase has any meaning. I'm not a physicist, but the creation of the warp bubble requires a huge amount of power, drawn in part from the collapse of three-dimensional space around it. That's how it was described.*

So the drive takes power by acting upon the space around it... using what as a power source? Night shook his head. *For all I know, your physics is better than mine, but how do you create a drive that powers itself by producing its result before it produces power to produce the result? Even quantum physics – what little I know of it – gets a headache over that one.*

I guess it's no more impossible than a plasma shuriken.

Oh, hells no. Night waved a dismissive paw. *The shuriken is easy to design, at least so far as my ideas...* He cut himself short. He had the sensation of "his body" looking around the cabin, just as he felt the tiger inside his mind look around at the pilot who's grim expression set on his muzzle with a certain amount of dread.

We have to get you out of here.

Yes. Night swallowed, or felt its equivalent. *I have to get back, find out how they managed to hook me into this thing. I have to... have to jump back into myself, or something like that. Do you know how?*

I don't think so. It's not like we swap out or anything. Is it?

I don't know. You've had experiences that I haven't, so I have to assume that you'll still be here when I go. You'll go back to being in your body.

My simulated body.

Night whispered, *Yes.*

Can someone just turn me off?

Kovach's face was as near stoic as anything Night had ever seen before. It was a request for information, if Night had any to provide. The tiger shook his head. *I don't know. I guess I'll be 'turned off' one day; everything dies, eventually.* He looked at the pilot, knowing that what he was doing wasn't real, knowing it was the *only* thing that was real. *I'll remember you. More than remember. You're in my head. In a way, we've merged, and I've led two lives. I'll take you with me.*

All I could ask for. Kovach grinned. *Unless you could program one hot night with Perryman into the system.*

I'd give you a lifetime together, if I could. Night smiled. *He's a sexy guy.*

Did you make up that line about juniper berries, or did I?

I'd be glad to credit you with that one.

Le Lapine Agile?

Sounds like a bordello above a French restaurant.

They shared something like a brief laugh, if only because they both needed it so much. After a moment, the pilot nodded. *Okay. How do we get you out of here?*

Trigger a recalibration. Seems to work best through some kind of shock or overload.

I have an idea, but you might not like it.

Night caught the brainwave and snorted. *Before you step up and punch me out, let's try something a little less Sam Spade.* He held out his arms to the pilot. *Two objects can't occupy the same space at the same time.*

We're not physical, like this, we're just—

Work with me here, tiger. This ain't my area of expertise; I'm improvising. I'm going to see if I can push you back into your body, there in the recliner, and use that force to catapult me out of here.

Think it'll work?

How in the multiple levels of hell am I supposed to know? Night spat. *I'm trying to outthink a simulation that is programmed to keep getting smarter, so that it can con information out of me. I'm just hoping I can will myself into getting out of it and back into myself, so that I can prevent this from happening again. On that much, we all agree.*

The pilot nodded, raising his arms. *At the risk of making a sexual entendre: Let's do it.*

Stepping forward, Night grabbed Kovach in a tight embrace. It was like grabbing hold of a live power conduit. Both shouted as if struck by a huge weight; Night had a sensation of the body in the recliner convulsing, the remains of a bottle of milk crashing to the deck of the ship's cabin (*sorry, mate, you'll have to clean that up*). He focused his mind on the image, the idea, the sensation that he wanted to make happen. He and Kovach shifted their forepaws, grabbed each other by the shoulders and began to spin around like crazed dancers in a centrifugal tarantella, eyes locked on each other, the sensation of building speed and power along with their thoughts, emotions, energies, elements, synergistically creating incredible energy.

KEEP 'EM GUESSING, FLYBOY

KEEP US SAFE, GENIUS

At the same moment, they released one another's shoulders. Night sensed Kovach landing back in his own body, utterly unsure if that statement had any basis in reality, while he sensed himself flying through everything and nothing, taking no time at all to move from where he was to where he found himself…

…in a recliner.

14

Night had a split second to feel his disappointment and disbelief, before screwing up his eyes and letting forth a yowl of pain. The return to the body contained a physical sensation, as if falling from a great height and slamming flat into the ground. Every inch of him vibrated, his fur shifting so violently that he wondered for a moment if he would actually shed every hair simultaneously. From tip to toe, he felt something ripple through him as if he were being pressed through a dough roller at a pizzeria.

His eyes snapped open. *Recalibration...*

Gasping, his muscles on fire, his nerves screaming at him, Night nevertheless managed the rictus of a death's-head grin through it all. The leather recliner was in his cabana at the resort, the living room area, all soft beige and off-white tones, track lighting, window open to the sea (feel the breeze, smell it, smell the salt), archway to the bedroom, neatly made, the bright golden bathroom beyond... He was *back.* He was himself again. He raised his paws to look at them (have you ever *really* looked at your paws, he thought with a touch of hysteria), realized that he really was back ("*I'm a REAL boy!*"). Night was unable to stop giggling for a full minute, from sheer relief. He was *back,* and by the gods, he intended to *stay* here.

He had a brief struggle getting out of the recliner. His muscles were definitely his, but it was if they weren't fully attached to himself. He was sore all over, and the realization brought another idea with him. Each successive recalibration had hurt more than the last. At first, it was a flicker, a sense of something rippling through him; it got worse each time he flipped between himself and the simulation. Remember that time in sick bay, when he actually tried to fight it, to stay in the massage room at the spa, instead of…

The tiger frowned. He had a memory of both sides of that recalibration. How…?

Have you forgotten me already?

"Kovach!" he said aloud. And like the memory of an old friend who had saved your bacon in the most dire of circumstances, the pilot seemed real enough to Night that he felt the grin on both their muzzles. Night, as a simulation, had absorbed the simulated pilot's information as well. Not exactly total recall, but enough for the tiger to feel as if he'd just been given a memory upgrade. Night wrapped his arms around himself, laughing. "I don't know if you can feel that, but consider yourself hugged."

And in his mind, he felt Kovach laughing with him.

Despite the soreness he experienced, Night never felt better in his life. Finally, he had some clear idea of what he had to do. Donovan first – he had to make sure the hyena would be out of danger before he could continue this. He looked around the suite, realizing that he'd made enough noise to bring the pup running to him to see what was wrong. Night frowned. Surely he left a note…?

The tiger's eyes lit upon his laptop, and he chuckled at the low-tech contrast of a paw-written note taped to the computer. He moved to retrieve the two, reading the hyena's scrawling yet attractive paw-writing: *Knowing that this device is a servant of evil, I opted to keep things simple. You seemed to be dozing, and I figured you needed it. Got my cell if you want to call/text; otherwise, see you for an early dinner? We can go for a slow sunset walk after, find a hidden cove in the gloaming, and do things that will frighten the fish. Love you – D.*

Night smiled. Here was another reason to fight to stay here. *Okay, Donovan,* he thought. *You win. When this crap is over with, you and I are going to get married, sell off everything, and start over somewhere.* The tiger shook his head. He wouldn't have believed he'd even think of such a thing. He was too independent. Even at Waveforce, he didn't always...

A frown crossed his face. Yeah. Work first. *His* work, not the company's.

He took the laptop to the desk near the sliding glass doors and booted up. The view beyond was beautiful, with as much pristine beach as could be possible after a resort had squatted itself in the middle of it. His laptop went through a succession of chimes, beeps, two-measure theme songs, and various other audible contortions until, finally, a single central command screen appeared for him to use. He had designed it himself, to be a master screen for all of his other open windows, the one window to rule them all.

Ears forward, concentration tensing his muscles slightly, the tiger sat in a desk chair that some Danish designer considered ergonomic and set his electronic minions to do his bidding. A tunneling VPN ensured his privacy; sniffers examined every bit and byte of his home servers, guarding against anything unauthorized, from cookies and seven-layer cakes to Trojans of any and all species. Locked up and prepared for attacks from any and all sides, Night tapped into a self-created IM system housed on his servers, sending a ping to an equally secure account. Several minutes later, he received a reply:

```
Queen to Queen's Level 3
```

Night smiled. Any Trekker worth his access to Memory Alpha would know the correct response, "Queen to King's Level 1." For this exchange, that would be dead wrong. He typed:

Your game is off, Rojan.

```
Are we secure?
```

My instruments say yes. What the hell is going on, Sodus?

```
I'm hoping you can tell me. Top brass is
looking for something, and the whisper says you
stole, or at least wiped out, some vital data.
What's that about?
```

No clue.

```
What happened to you, anyway? We know you were
sent on a vacation, because of all that medical
crap, but now that you're gone, it's Conspiracy
Central at the office.
```

Night rubbed his forehead briefly. He needed more information, but he didn't know what the information was, nor who could give it to him. "Hijacked." The word still echoed in his mind. He wasn't even entirely sure what that meant. Somehow, someone had figured out a way to inject him directly into a simulation without his being fully aware of it. And that required a lot more sophisticated stuff than he was working on. He tapped out a question to Sodus:

Tell me about the simulations we've been working on. The Kabura-Ya.

```
What about it?
```

Do we have the entire project, or is there another department working on it part of it?

```
I oversee the development of the gaming
aspects. There are probably applications that I'm
not privy to.
```

Military applications?

```
It's tech. Brass Hats love their toys.
```

That's why missiles look like they do. The Preparation H-Bomb – guaranteed to shrink world problems.

Ew.

What part of the project would they be using?

...and I should know about this, why?

The game we're designing has two things that attract most gamers: Immersion and violence. For the folks who don't get enough sadistic pleasure from having plants kill zombies, we're creating whole new weapons, and whole new ways to practice deploying them. But it's still a game. How would that have military applications?

A paper clip has military applications. Anything we can think up, they can use somehow. The question is whether or not they can actually build it.

How much limitation is that?

Almost none, these days. That which the mind can conceive, it can achieve.

Night shivered, remembering what the Sarge had said in the simulation – that the tech exists, but the concept doesn't. He had dreamed up the plasma shuriken, the Bradbury Drive, and who knew what else that he'd jotted ideas for. The last thing he wanted was to have it made real.

Night?

Still here. Sodus, how dangerous is this stuff really?

Depends on what you mean by "real." We specialize in fantasy, Night – games, fun, play-time. If someone wants to make Hell real, it's not our call.

What if we got stuck in Hell?

???

Simulations. The Kobura-Ya still requires external equipment, doesn't it?

Of course. Simulations are voluntary.

What if they weren't? Could there be a way to… let's use the word "hijack" someone's mind and put it into a simulation?

After an extremely long pause, words appeared: Let us fervently pray that there is not.

And if the mind could conceive…?

A soft, low, disconcerting sound from the computer's speaker interrupted Night's thoughts. In the lower right corner of the master screen, three small hexagons bearing the letters M, C, and B, glowed softly green. At the inside edge of the C hexagon, a small red dot flashed.

Location?

Home.

You're being tapped.

The line is clean.

Caspar is under attack. Dissolving link, executing countermeasures. Contact later. Laputan Machine.

Paws flashing across the keyboard, Night ended his conversation and set to reinforcing the protections around his home server farm. Like most sneak thieves, whatever was trying to get past his firewalls cut its own connection as soon as he set tracers on it. His faithful electronic hounds returned no further information, but the intruder was given a metaphorical bite on the ass. That thought, perversely, made him think both about eating and about biting an ass he was particularly fond of. He let go a snort, shook his head a little. Perhaps it was closer to dinnertime than he thought. He had the sudden desire to find Donovan and try to quit thinking about this mess for awhile.

The trilling of the house phone surprised him. He knew the hyena had his cell, so who…? Night moved to the small table near the sofa and picked up the receiver.

"Hello, the is the concierge calling." The accent was a perfect BRP, the supposed pinnacle of the vocal expression of English. It never failed to make Night think of the seventh son of a British butler who had, like all of his forefathers, been a faithful retainer of some centuries-old aristocracy. "Is this Mr. O'Connell?"

"Yes."

"Just wanted to remind you of your hot stone massage booking at four this afternoon… if that's still convenient, sir?"

"Ye-es," he hesitated slightly. "That's with Gemini, isn't it?"

"Yes sir, room nine in the main spa. Enjoy!"

Night hung up the phone. "Not necessarily the word I'd have used."

15

"Now what do we do?" Night whispered to the empty suite.

Want a minority opinion? Kovach piped up in Night's mind.

Kovach?

You got someone else roaming around in this brain that I haven't met yet?

Not that I know of. Smiling softly, the tiger nodded. *Bring it.*

The voice in his head continued. *My life – if I may call it that – is steeped in military training, with all of the knowledge and heuristic models of defensive combat. My idea, then, is that you're under attack, and we need to keep you safe. You've seen an attack on your server farm, so your information is under attack. Your company seems to think that you've compromised information, so your job is under attack. You've had yourself hijacked into a full-model simulation without your consent, so you, personally, are under attack. Unless I'm greatly mistaken, or your middle name is Job and God wants a re-match, these things are linked directly. There's one enemy, attacking on three fronts. To keep you safe, we need to know who your friends are. Forgive me, I have to ask: What about Donovan?*

Night shook his head hard. *No. He's not part of it, and I don't want him to be. If necessary, we need to send him home, to keep him out of this.*

Kovach seemed to hug him. *Okay, Night. Let's take that as gospel and move on. Sodus?*

Project Coordinator at Waveforce. He's probably got his fingers in a lot of pies, but I can't believe he'd actively try to hurt me. His job is to protect our program from the High Upstairs. He's in charge of making the Kabura-Ya work, getting the finished product made. He makes the rest of us minions dance the tune.

What about his superiors? Does he have to dance to their tune? Could they want something out of you?

That's the sum of the hints from Sodus. What it is that they want, I don't know.

Could it be the shuriken, or the Bradbury Drive?

Night shook his head wearily. *I don't know how, or why. I'm no physicist; I can't control space and time, and come up with some kind of super-weapon. The things only work in simulation anyway.*

Okay, so Sodus is probably okay, but he should be watched in case his masters are making him do something against his will.

I do so love conspiracy theories.

My keen sense of detection tells me that you're being sarcastic. And don't ask – I've been sparring with Perryman for a while now. Okay, what about Gemini? Do we go see him, or avoid him?

You're the defense coordinator; what's your recommendation?

The undeniable sense of a wry and wholly self-satisfied smile on Kovach's face set the tone for his next words: *What they don't know can hurt them a lot.*

* * * * *

Night, clad once more only in a towel, knocked gently on the door with the number "9" on it, and was amused to see that the ornament had been fixed; it stayed in place. A familiar voice from within called to him, and he went inside.

The room seemed exactly as he left it, candles, wood paneling, ambient music and all. As with the last time, Gemini was facing away from him at first. The difference now, as the tiger closed the door behind him, was that the wolf turned and greeted him by name. "Night! Very good to see you again. I can only guess I did something right last time, for you to return so soon."

"It's good to take advantage of whatever perks the facility offers," Night managed what he hoped was a disarming smile. "Never know when I might be back here."

"Good point," Gemini laughed. He shook Night's paw by reaching across the massage table, then waved a paw at it saying, "Assume the position."

"And I thought you weren't supposed to solicit your customers."

"For you, I'd make an exception. Now lie down and behave."

"How about a change this time? Have you got the headrest and the forearm props where you can get to them?"

The young wolf paused, his eyes flickering in slight confusion, but he nodded readily enough. "Sure. Weren't you comfortable last time?"

"Sure. Just wanted to see if maybe the other way worked better."

"Okay. I'll set it up."

It took only a matter of moments, during which time Night felt Kovach nodding his approval. With the headrest in place, the bulk of Night's body would be laid flat on the table. Granted, he would only be able to see a small area of the floor under him and nothing else, but his ears were still sharp. The forearm rests would provide a better point of leverage than having his forepaws bunched under his chin. If the masseur tried to climb atop him again to hold him down, this positioning would put the odds of escape more in Night's favor. When everything was in place, Gemini patted the table and nodded. "Good to go."

Night removed his towel and lay naked upon the table, placing his forehead on the far end of the padded ring, his forearms where they belonged on either side of him. He forced his tail to relax and not betray his unease. Inside his mind, Kovach reminded him that they'd discussed this, reviewed the contingency plan that they had concocted. In only moments, the wolf's paws began their masterful work on Night's bunched shoulders. If the plan was to work, the tiger had to relax and stay alert at the same time. Something in his mind remembered commercials for coffee some years ago, and the connection almost made him laugh.

"Good grief, tiger," Gemini said. "Something must have gotten you pretty upset since our last visit. These muscles feel as tight as cord wood."

"I had considered visiting the steam room before I came here." His voice was slightly muffled to him, as it had to bounce off the carpeted floor. "I wasn't sure if that would be relaxing or invigorating."

"Depends on the company you keep." The masseur's smile was evident in his voice. "We had to post a sign reminding the users that vigorous exercise in the steam room could lead to dehydration, exhaustion, and fainting. One client commented that he was here for precisely those objectives."

"Takes all kinds." Inside his mind, Night sensed Kovach sniggering. He was distracted by Gemini once again working his strong-pawed magic along the length of his spinal cord. Night uttered something between a grunt and a deep purr, surprising himself and Gemini as well.

"You okay?"

"Yeah. I guess I just really needed this. Didn't mean to be quite so vocal about it."

"I'm flattered. I haven't even gotten to the stones yet."

"That's because I'm lying on my stomach."

Night felt the gentle tap of a reproving finger on the back of his head as Gemini laughed. "Flirt! You're going to cost me my job. You ready for hot stones? The massage kind, before you get another smart answer in your head."

"Too late. But yes, I'd love to have the stones again. You want me completely relaxed, don't you?"

"Well, that *is* my job, after all."

One of them, Kovach wised off in Night's head. *Still with me, genius?*

Never left, flyboy. "Must get a bit tedious, sometimes. Customer service has its limitations."

Night felt the first stone applied to his spine, rubbing slowly and firmly down to his tail. "Actually, I kind of like it," Gemini said. "I get to meet all kinds of interesting people. You, for instance."

"What makes me so interesting?"

"Your job, for one – game design sounds so cool." The wolf placed another stone carefully, moving and speaking slowly, calmly. "I'm not a complete nerd, but I do enjoy various RPGs from time to time. And I haven't met that many people with such a complete knowledge of sixties television shows."

Sloppy segue, Kovach observed.

"Ever see one called *Checkmate*? Sebastian Cabot in the lead, and Doug McClure when he was a Boy Scout." Night chuckled. "They were a detective agency that was supposed to be able to stop a crime before it happened. Very cool stuff for its day. Ton of great guest stars."

"Must have missed that one," Gemini said softly. "Sounds good, though." He placed the last stone up between Night's shoulder blades. "That should feel nice and comfy."

"Oh, it's lovely," the tiger whispered, his muscles relaxed, but his mind staying sharp, thanks to Kovach's careful watch over things. *He'll make his move soon. Get ready.*

Last time, I thought he was going to dry-hump me or something.

Quit dreaming and focus.

Night felt a sheet being draped over him – something new, but non-threatening, at least so far. "To help keep in the warmth for a bit," the wolf explained. "You just lay there and melt."

"I like that idea."

Legs and hindpaws appeared in the tiger's limited frame of vision, his head resting on the padded circular headrest poking out of the table proper. The legs folded, and most of Gemini's body came in to view. "There," the wolf said. "We can talk for a minute. Unless you'd rather doze off."

"Talking's good."

Taking a deep breath, Gemini said softly, "You are Number Six."

Night smiled. "I am not a number; I am a free spirit."

It would be impossible to exaggerate the look of pure shock on the wolf's face. Night only wished that he'd had a camera.

"Holy gods," Gemini finally managed to breathe. "You've broken through!"

"Apparently," the tiger smiled. "I only wish that I knew what it is that I've broken, and through what."

"If I'm right, you've broken the hijacking entirely."

"Hijack. That's what your twin brother called it. Except he's not your brother, is he? He's a simulation, even though he doesn't know it."

Somberly, Gemini nodded. "The *Heartwielder* simulation is massive. The PC cloaks were the only way that some of us have been able to sneak into it. I wasn't able to inject myself directly into the simulation, so I created a character that looked like me, hoping that I could contact you when you were hijacked into it."

"You're a fabricator?"

"Not technically. I help create the backgrounds for characters; someone else does the programming."

"Whoever it is, they're good. Everyone in the simulation thinks that they're real."

"We had to do it that way." Gemini looked sad. "At first, it was a way to protect you. We thought that you might succumb to the idea that you were a simulation yourself. Instead, we tried to create a way to make you think that your mind had been hijacked into a living being, a fabricated clone so to speak."

"Wait a minute," Night waved a paw gently in the air as if erasing a chalkboard. "Who's this 'we,' paleface?"

"You won't like it."

"Shock, horror, imagine my surprise."

Gemini paused, sighed. "The government calls us cyber-terrorists. We're as patriotic as any sane person might be, and we don't advocate violence. We're trying to get the military to come clean about its weapons development. We called ourselves the Sixth Wall – giving transparency to the Pentagon."

"Like 'breaking the fourth wall' in drama."

"It also makes a hexagon, which may hold six trigrams and a *taijitu* in the middle." Responding to Night's furrowed brows, Gemini explained, "You know, what people call the yin-yang symbol?" He sighed again. "Yeah, pretentious as hell, isn't it?"

I may not be as perceptive as you, Kovach said inside Night's head, *but he sounds just a little too crazy to be a good liar. It may or may not be real, but it's true so far as he knows.*

"Forgive me asking, but does the government really think you're a threat?"

The wolf blushed, both offended and embarrassed. "We're not loony-tunes. That part of it became a game, because it pissed off the FBI when some of us started chanting mantras and meditations when we were being questioned. We're hackers, but overall, we don't do anything but try to look where they don't want us to look. It's how we found you in the first place."

"What do you mean?"

"Waveforce isn't pristine, Night. I'm sorry to tell you, but our research tells us that the military is all over that company."

It was Night's turn to sigh. "I can't say I'm surprised there, either. Whatever you guys programmed into the simulation, your characters – especially your would-be twin – put forward some good arguments for thinking that the game research is a cover to come up with the weirdest kinds of weapons we can think of, so that the Brass Hats can tell their people what to build. The scientists have to make it real, but it takes us twisted creative types to come up with the ideas."

"Wait…" Gemini shook his head. "You got that from the simulation?"

"Yeah. Your twin and the Sarge took me to some dive to give me the dirt."

"Who's Sarge?"

"The big old bulldog feller who's in charge of…" Night broke off, raising his head out of the headrest to look directly into Gemini's eyes. "War games. The Phibriglex-62 simulation. And something tells me you didn't program any of that."

The wolf stood quickly. "Hope you've relaxed enough, Night – we need to get you out of here, right now."

16

Back in Night's cabana, Gemini waited somewhat impatiently as the tiger set up the laptop to try his communication with Sodus once more. He needed information, right from the source. The answers had to lie in the game simulation that he'd been working on. The clues lay in all of the references he had put into the program from his favorite time period, the British TV stuff, even the reference to Phibriglex-62. That part of the program was supposed to be for a warm-up to the new gamer. The briefing was a "cut scene," as it's known in the video gaming world – a miniature movie to move the storyline forward. After the briefing, which in this case included instructions on the controls of the Starhawk fighter (a tutorial for the gamer new to this particular game), there followed an in-game simulation designed to give the "new recruit" a little practice in handling the controls. Night had used Phibriglex-62 as a tribute and a tease, hoping that the gamers would actually be curious enough to learn a little history as they played their game.

The game itself required a large number of characters, both Player Characters and Non-Player Characters. PCs were "shells" or "cloaks" for players to adopt – Kovach, for example. A gamer could play the part of Kovach, just as it seemed Night had been doing. Non-Player Characters (NPCs) were less complicated, and to give them some semblance of a personality without doing too much research and planning, Night would often turn to people from his own life, just to serve as basic outlines. Sarge, based upon a gym-teacher-cum-drill-instructor for his high school

ROTC group, was one of the NPCs in this game, with limited range and pre-determined sets of responses to what the PCs were doing. Or, as Night now ruefully realized, that was what he was when he had been created. The character of Sarge had been manipulated, or perhaps turned into a kind of PC, being used by someone else, just as Gemini had used the nurse character in the simulation to inject himself into the scenario.

For a brief moment, Night felt the presence of Kovach in his mind, as if the tiger were looking over his shoulder, watching the explanations unfold. A wave of guilt washed over him, and he looked to Kovach apologetically. A little surprisingly, the pilot shook his head, smiling a little. *I have to learn. I have to know what you know, if I'm going to help.*

I'm sorry, I didn't mean –

Kovach held up a forestalling paw. *I'm strong, stubborn, focused, just like you made me. Keep going. We've got to get you safe first, or we're both going to be switched off.*

Sighing a little, Night looked over his shoulder at Gemini. "Exactly how fast do we need to get out of here?"

"Depends on who's looking," the wolf said. "Personally, I'd pack up and take a plane to anywhere but home, just as soon as possible. If I can get in touch with some of my contacts, maybe I could arrange a place for you to stay."

"What about Donovan?"

"Both of you, of course. Have you texted him?"

"He should be here soon." Night shook his head, sighing. "I have no idea what to tell him."

"Start with telling him that you love him." Gemini smiled softly. "If I'm reading your situation right, he needs to know that before he'll believe any of this."

The tiger nodded slowly, his paws flying over the keyboard, opening the tunneling VPN and regaining a secure connection to his home computer. He sent a ping to Sodus and waited for the answer. "Have you been spying on us?"

"No, not like that. I observed the two of you here at the resort, and we picked up on you two as an item long before this mess happened. You've been together for a while; it shows in your social media, whether you knew it or not. I have to admit to just a touch of jealousy. You make a great couple."

Night smiled. "Seems like everyone knows that but me. But you're right. I want him kept safe, above all."

"Sounds like love to me."

A noise from the computer caught Night's ear. He looked at the message on the screen and frowned:

```
Queen to Queen's Level 3
```

Gemini hovered over the tiger's shoulder, then thought better of it. "I'm sorry; I should know better than to watch."

"Not a problem, at the moment. What's the countersign?"

The wolf shrugged. "If I remember my *Trek* trivia properly, it's Queen to King's Level 1."

"But any Trekker would know that, so I chose something similar but different. The countersign is a line from another episode where 3-D chess is played. Makes the pairing unique."

"Good idea."

"Except that this is wrong."

"What do you mean?"

Night stared at the screen. "Just before I logged off last time, my sniffers found an intruder in my server farm. My last message to Sodus gave a code key for the next meeting, but he should be the only one to know it."

"What did you say?"

"I said, 'Laputan Machine.'"

Gemini shook his head. "Don't know that one."

"Not a fan of *Gulliver's Travels*?" Night grinned.

The computer dinged again: `Repeat, Queen to Queen's Level 3`

"Every secure contact needs both a code and a key," the tiger continued. "The key tells you which code sign and countersign to use next time. 'Laputan Machine' refers to Jonathan Swift, but also to the very popular video game *Deus Ex*. It's a kill code, and it too has an expected response – 'Flatlander Woman' – which would be incorrect and let me know that the sender isn't who he says he is. The problem is, Sodus should be using that code sign to contact me, not the *Trek* reference."

The wolf's eyes danced. "So you think this is an imposter?"

"Got to be. Sodus knows better than to use the same code key that we used when the sniffers were activated."

"What happens if you give the matched line instead of the correct countersign?"

"It should shut down both sides of the IM connection, on first use; that forces the imposter to reset his connection, which I can see. It buys me time as well as a chance to nab his IP address, if I'm lucky. If he's stubborn enough to try it a second time, using the matched line not only terminates the connection, it locks the door – the original code sign won't even get to me, and the sender will discover that he's allowed a very nasty kill code to break right through his firewall."

"I like your thinking." Gemini paused. "Test it."

Night, following the wolf's idea, nodded and typed: `Queen to King's Level 1`

After only a moment, new words appeared: `Invalid Response, Repeat, Queen to Queen's Level 3`

"Is that a correct response?"

"No." Night frowned. "There should be no response at all. My messaging screen should have deactivated, and his too. And he responded too quickly; there was no time lag. He should have had to take at least a few extra seconds to reset his connection."

"This tells us two things. That isn't your contact..."

"...and someone's hacked my system." The tiger's paws moved swiftly over the keyboard, activating response programs and bringing up status information. The three hexagons that represented his servers, all normally solid green, showed one hexagon completely red and another partially so. "Caspar is compromised; Melchior is under attack, but Balthazar seems secure at the moment."

The wolf smirked. "The three wise men. Cute."

"Beats Larry, Curly, and Moe." Night struggled furiously with his readouts and commands. "If they breach the whole farm, they'll own it."

"Do you have a redundant system?"

"In theory, yes."

"What does that mean?"

"Each of the three servers has a backup server, an identical computer from chips to RAID. Every thirty minutes, the servers backup to their respective machines. In the event of failover, there's a seventh machine that does nothing but hold the IP space open. If there's an error on the main farm, failover reroutes all incoming requests to the seventh machine, ostensibly until the backup servers can be brought online. That allows repair to the main servers while the mirror handles new information. When it's fixed, we reverse it all – restore to the seventh machine, copy over the backups to restore the mains, then bring the mains back online. Keeps everything available whenever I need it."

"Is the failover automatic?"

"Usually. But to answer your question more completely…" Night entered a string of information and instructions into his main window and pressed ENTER. "…that would mean that my backups would be online after they've gotten control of my main servers. To fix that, we have three steps. I've just shut down the backup to the failover farm."

The screen glowed: CONFIRMED

"Step Two: Disconnect the failover computer from the backup server farm." More keys.

CONFIRMED

"Step Three: Prometheus." More keys.

ARE YOU SURE? Y/N

Night didn't hesitate to press Y.

"This won't take too long."

"What exactly did you just do?"

The tiger looked up at the wolf. "The Prometheus kill code is lethal indeed. I've just over-clocked my CPU circuits to 250%, turned off the temperature monitors, and just to make matters even more deadly, deactivated both the computer fans and the server room air conditioning. Those computers will be nothing but melted slag in a very few minutes." Anticipating the wolf's question, Night said, "No, the failover and backup computers are in a completely separate facility, with their own controls. They're not even at my house."

After a long pause, during which Gemini's expression didn't alter a whit, he finally said, "You're the kind of guy I really like to hang out with."

"I'll take that as a compliment." Night smiled, then sighed. "We're on our own now. No help from anyone at the company."

"That might turn out to be a good thing. This guy you were supposed to talk to, what's his name?"

"Sodus Busby. He's the project coordinator. The only folks above him are company directors."

"So he's Number Two?"

The tiger's eyes opened wide, and his jaw dropped slightly. "Oh gods, I sincerely hope not."

Gemini put a paw to Night's shoulder, his ears slightly splayed. "I'm sorry. The thought just sort of slipped out. Maybe it's not him. Or maybe he's being used. Forget about it for now – we're probably better off without the connection. One more thing: Is there anything on the laptop that someone else would want?"

"No, but there's nothing like being safe." He unplugged the laptop from the wall and took it into the bathroom. There, he began running water in the large beige-tinted tub. "I hate wasting good hardware, but there's nothing on here that I can't recreate. And that includes my record time for solving a Free Cell game." As the tub filled up, he set the open laptop on the floor of the tub and let the water rush over it. Since it was still turned on at the time, some fairly impressive sparks leapt up, which rather surprised him. When it had all stopped, he raised up a hind paw and smashed a heel into the keyboard, exposing more of the equipment below to the rising water.

Standing in the doorway, the wolf observed, "You really ought to leave a bigger tip for the maids, you know."

"Remind me as we're checking out."

"What do you mean, checking out?"

Wolf and tiger turned to see a young hyena with a confused and mildly frightened look on his face enter the cabana by the sliding glass doors. Night sighed with relief and moved to take Donovan into his arms and hold him closely. "I'm glad you're back, love."

"Night, what is going on here? What happened to your laptop?"

The tiger cupped the hyena's face gently in his paws and kissed him. The hyena smelled of sea breeze, the ginger and lime soap used at the resort, and just the faintest hint of his own musk, a combination that Night's brain locked in so tightly that he actually shivered slightly. He looked the pup deeply in the eyes and said, "We'd better sit down, Donovan. This could take a while."

17

As Night steered the hyena to the sofa, Kovach's voice popped up in his head. *So, that's the amazing Donovan, eh? Definitely cute.*

Cool yer jets, flyboy; this one's mine.

I could tell by the way his scent rang every bell in your belfry. I promise not to hang around if you two get frisky. An idea for you, though. Don't tell him about me – Gemini is still here. I know you trust Donovan, but even though Gemini knows you've "broken through," he may not know that I'm actually part of you now. Let's keep that as the ace in the hole.

Good thinking.

Paranoia has its value.

Donovan took Night's forepaws in his own, his face a mask of worry. "Okay. Whatever it is, I'm ready. What's going on?"

"Introductions first." The tiger nodded toward the wolf who sat in a nearby chair. "This is Gemini. He's a masseur here at the spa. And in what might be called another life, he's a nurse onboard a starship called *Heartwielder*."

"What the hell!" the hyena growled, yanking his paws from Night's grasp. "I've been scared out of my wits over you for weeks, and you come in with some damned game crap…"

Night gripped Donovan by his shoulders. "Exactly, love. That's what I'm telling you. There's more to the game than I ever thought. No, it's not reality, and no, I'm not crazy. But within that game environment, in that simulation, something really insane is going on. And somehow, I've been dragged into it, literally."

"And how does this guy fit into it?" Donovan asked with a bit of bite in his voice.

"I know you're not much of a gamer, luv, so let me explain what a 'cloak' is. In a total sensory immersion game, where you feel like you're actually inside the simulation, you have to have a sort of shell or cloak for the programmers to let other non-player characters interact with. It's like putting on a cloak, or a glove, in order to move around inside the program. Gemini's character is a nurse onboard a starship. Clear so far?"

"No, but it's consistent." Donovan snorted, shook his head. He took a breath and exhaled sharply, looking into Night's eyes. The tiger saw what he'd always seen, and what he was foolish enough to think that he wasn't falling in love with over all these months. That was a mistake he intended to remedy, just as soon as he could get out of this insanity. "Okay… is there a beginning to this story?"

"I'll give it a try…"

* * * * *

It was a good hour before Donovan had enough grasp of the story both to understand it and to not think the tiger had gone completely insane. "So bottom line, I was right about Waveforce," he said. "I didn't want you going back, and I want it even less now." He shook his head. "I still can't understand how they could just pull your mind into the computer like that."

"It should be impossible, unless..." Night sighed. "I hate conspiracy theories, but... I'm wondering if they implanted something when I was in hospital."

Donovans' eyes looked like saucers. "Oh gods...! How, when?"

"I don't know. But I was unconscious for a few days, so—"

"You were comatose, hooked up to every machine I'd ever seen. I stayed with you every moment that I could. It must have happened before then."

"That would make sense," Gemini said. "The usual equipment to jack into a simulation is external, using various monitoring equipment that..." He chuckled. "I'm sorry. Might be easier if I just showed you my headgear. That's how I got into the *Heartwielder* simulation to find you. It's back in my cabana."

"They must have come up with some kind of wetware." Night saw Donovan's confused expression. "It's a term originally coined for cyberpunk fiction. It means hardware that's designed to be fused with a person's body, usually the brain."

The hyena was astonished. "Does that stuff actually exist?"

"Probably. Most likely, some military Dr. Frankenstein has created prototypes. Whatever the case, I need to get my head examined."

Despite the tension, or because of it, the trio laughed. Even Kovach, inside Night's head, joined in. *Not that I'd know,* he thought to Night, *but I don't see anything in here. Well, okay, nothing that shouldn't be here.*

Funny, flyboy.

Hey, I try.

"Okay," Donovan said at last. "This is not what I signed up for, Night, but I'm not going to leave you behind. So if you're going to try pulling one of those 'I want you out of harm's way' scenes, you can stuff it. I'll start by getting us packed." The hyena moved quickly from the couch, paused to kiss Night on his forehead, then padded into the bedroom to get started.

"I'll call the concierge," Gemini offered. "He should be able to get you guys on a flight out of here quickly enough. Family emergency, Salt Lake City."

Night frowned. "I don't have—"

"Sixth Wall. I've got people there. I'll contact them in advance and follow on as soon as I can get out of here."

The house phone rang. Night flicked a glance at Gemini and waved him off. "Don't let anyone know you were here. Go see the concierge in person; tell him I learned about the emergency during my massage with you, and you've volunteered to help out."

"You got it." The wolf moved toward the sliding glass doors and stopped dead in his tracks.

Night picked up the phone. "Yes?"

"Mr. O'Connell?" The perfect BRP was unmistakable, identifying the caller even before he did so for himself. "This is the concierge; how may I be of assistance?"

The tiger's eyes widened, and he looked back to Gemini, who stood motionless – literally, utterly motionless – at the sliding glass doors, one paw in front of the other in such a way that he shouldn't have been able to balance at all. "I received some bad news from home; I'm going to have to cut the vacation a little short, I'm afraid." He waved at Gemini. The wolf was still as a statue.

"Oh, I'm very sorry to hear that, sir. May I assist you in arranging transport?"

"Yes, that would be very helpful." Night carried the cordless phone back into the bedroom, where he saw that Donovan had begun packing. The suitcases and duffels were on the bed, some clothes already in them. Donovan stood at the closet, reaching up to take out some of the clothing that had been placed on hangars. The hyena was stubbornly meticulous about certain things, something just short of the gay cliché of "fussy," a fact that Night had known from long ago. He stood now, digitigrade to get something from a top shelf. He stood as still and unmoving as Gemini in the next room. Night had the sudden gut-sinking feeling that, if a breeze blew up around him, Donovan's fur wouldn't move the slightest bit.

"Where would you like to go?" asked the polished, professional voice on the phone.

Night swallowed. "Salt Lake City. I need to go to Salt Lake City."

"Really, sir? I thought you were from the Midwest, Iowa perhaps, or Kansas."

"Extended family," Night said, with a prompt from Kovach. *Keep 'em talking, genius, until we figure out what sort of crap we've landed in.*

"Very good, sir, let me just check with the airport."

Night ran back into the living room. Gemini had not moved, not so much as twitched an ear. The wolf's eyes were bright and clear, yet they seemed to see nothing. The tiger went to the sliding glass doors and looked outside. Donovan had arrived no more than an hour ago, when it was still only late afternoon; by rights, the sun should be setting soon. Instead, outside was darkness, full night, clear calm skies with the occasional billowy cloud scudding across the crescent moon. The resort area looked peaceful, a few indistinct figures walking along the shoreline not too far away, the moon full enough in the untroubled sky to give a little light but not much clarity. As Night watched, the couple on the shoreline passed behind a building, beyond his vision, only to reappear at the far end of the beach to walk upon the same sands that they had traversed a moment ago.

"I'm terribly sorry, sir; there seems to be some difficulty at the airport. Planes have been grounded for a time. Probably the weather."

The storm outside the cabana looked harsh, not enough to worry anyone safe and snug indoors, but he could see how smaller planes – the commuter planes that would use the local landing strip – might not want to venture out in it. By the look of it, the squall clearly had been raging for some time.

"Yes, of course." Night's voice was slow and not quite his own. Inside his mind, Kovach watched with dawning comprehension and a horrid idea that struck him dumb with disbelief.

"Perhaps I could suggest another location, sir?"

"I'm sure that you could. I'd really like to go to Salt Lake City, though."

"And how many of us could say that with such sincerity, sir? No, I have a much better location for you. Safe from the storms, and there's so much to do there. You'd never get bored on such a big ship."

"You're booking me on the Love Boat?" Night went into the bathroom, the medium-sized bathroom with the powder blue tile and fixtures. The tub was dry as a bone, and his laptop seemed in perfect condition.

"Nothing so prosaic, sir."

"You hacked my laptop."

"Whyever would you think such a thing? There's nothing on it that we didn't put there. It's as much a part of this simulation as you are."

Inside Night's mind, Kovach screamed his disbelief in desperate monosyllables. "What makes you think you can just yank me back there?"

"We can't. You've broken the lock that we had on you. But we have other tools at our disposal. Have a look in the bedroom."

Stumbling into the room, the tiger looked at Donovan, stripped naked and strapped to the bed, tied, gagged, arms and legs spread wide, a look of sheer terror on his face. Night swallowed, felt Kovach with him, both trying to focus on the same conclusion. "This is a simulation," Night said slowly. "There's nothing you can do to him, or me."

"Perhaps. Or perhaps not. Suppose that we had him hooked into the simulation directly. He would still feel. That's why it's called total immersion. Pain is still pain."

Donovan's body convulsed, appearing to be struck repeatedly by invisible fists. Welts, abrasions, cuts appeared on him in a dozen places at once.

"STOP IT!" Night screamed, hurling the phone to the floor and running to the bed. He threw himself over Donovan's body to protect him, reacting viscerally, as they knew he would. He had no reason to think that he could protect a simulated body this way, his own or Donovan's. But it's how he would react in the real world, and that was what they counted on. He tried to force his breathing to slow, tried to make himself think. Inside his mind, Kovach seemed to have retreated slightly into the shadows, outside of the spotlight, ears splayed, his eyes round with horror.

"Shall we talk now?"

The voice did not come from the phone any longer. It didn't have to. "What is it you want?"

"I think you know."

"You want me to go back to the *Heartwielder* simulation."

"More. We want you to fix the Phibriglex-62 simulation."

"Fix it how?"

"Make it work. Make it … doable."

"And if I can't?"

"Oh you can, Mr. O'Connell. Because you're that bright. That clever. And you wouldn't want your exotic little playtoy to be hurt any further, would you?" The voice seemed to think for a moment. "We've never actually killed someone in a simulation. Not a PC anyway. We do wonder what that would do to the subject. I've been told there was a television show that asked the same question…"

"You've made your point!" Night snarled. He got up off the bed and started untying Donovan.

"Poor, poor Mr. O'Connell." The voice dripped with faintly amused condescension that could only be properly brewed in a vat of wealth, privilege, and centuries of self-entitlement. "What *are* you doing?"

"You want me to cooperate, I want him safe and as comfortable as possible. I want him – and his simulation – pampered. I want Gemini to look after him."

"Not possible," the voice said. "We've locked him out of the simulation permanently. He's a hacker, found his way in without access, trying to take you away from us. But you see, Mr. O'Connell, we own you. You will give us what we want, or we'll leave you in here for as long as it takes. You won't see anything even close to the 'real world.' We can replay the scenario as many times as we wish. We control your 'cloak' enough to make sure that he shows up at every repetition. Over and over and over again, until you give us what we want."

Tenderly, Night removed the gag from Donovan's mouth and held the hyena as the pup collapsed in his arms and cried. "Don't do it, Night, whatever it is, don't do it. I don't want you going back there."

The tiger shushed and soothed as best he could. It was an illusion, but at the moment, it was all he could have for himself. "I'll come back to you. I don't know how, but I'll come back. I promised you that. The real you."

Donovan sobbed for a few moments, then kissed Night feverishly, looked him in the eye. "Come back to me, my tiger. My genius tiger, come back to me."

"I will. I swear it." Night looked into the simulated eyes, as if searching for something. *"Was wilst du? Lebensraum?"* he asked softly.

"Of course I do," the hyena responded.

Slowly, Night nodded and gently slipped himself free of the hyena's grasp. He stood and addressed the room generally. "You'd better hope that I can still function when you recalibrate me again. The last one nearly tore my head off."

"Don't fight it so much. You should be able to afford one or two more before the trauma to your mind affects your physical brain too much. We just have to slip you into Kovach's 'cloak' once more. If you'll stay there, you'll probably be safe enough."

"You damage me, you don't get what you want."

"And neither will anyone else," said the voice. "It's second best, but it's better than nothing. Now… sit in the recliner. It will hurt less if you relax."

Night moved slowly, padding back into the living room. Gemini had vanished. The storm outside, no longer needed, had been replaced by the endless loop of the distant couple walking along the shore edge. *Default idle,* the programmer part of him labeled it. After as much delay as he could get away with, he finally came to rest in the leather recliner, his tail carefully arranged, kicking back to the half-reclined position. "Can I have another hot stone massage? They really worked wonders."

The world exploded into light, noise, and pain.

18

"HOLD HIM DOWN!"

Night was barely aware of his surroundings, the excruciating pain jagging through his mind allowing only the dimmest input. Someone forced his muzzle open and wedged some kind of padded stick between his teeth. He knew that his jaw had clamped down on it, but he had no control over it. His body was convulsing violently, his arms flailing, his hind paws scrabbling for purchase on some kind of table or hard surface underneath him. Several people around him, trying to hold him flat. A stench in the air, a sense of something hot flowing… his bladder had let go entirely. He thought he felt a needle in his arm, but there was no room in his thoughts for anything but the agony of feeling his mind being vivisected by a chainsaw.

Orders. Responses. Clothing being ripped and cut away from him. The pain and convulsions slowly fading over a matter of minutes.

"I think he's coming around, doctor."

"Kovach?" The tiger heard the voice, the familiar voice of Doc Hazlitt, and was momentarily surprised that he was wanting to answer from two different places. He felt a gentle paw caressing his head. "Kovach, if you can understand me, don't try to answer, just listen. You've had a grand mal seizure; we don't know why. There's a padded splint in your muzzle, to keep you from biting your tongue off. We gave you a whopper of a sedative,

134

Phenobarbital if you're interested; when it takes hold, you should feel a lot more relaxed, body and mind. When that relaxation kicks in, we can take out the splint. Your heart's strong, your breathing's good – you're gonna be okay. You're in good paws, son, just relax."

Somewhere in his head, the tiger began forming coherent thought again, and from that began to feel that sense of being in two places, more like being two people... *Kovach?*

His mind feeling fragmented, first from the adrenal rush and now from the slowly growing strength of the anticonvulsant drug, the tiger fought to reassemble the shattered pieces of his mind. He had an image of a small, dark room, of a kind of spotlight shining down from overhead, of being two people yet one person, saw himself yet saw someone else...

Night? I hope that's you and not some drug-induced side-effect.

That's my line, flyboy. Are you thinking any better than I am?

I don't see how.

Why are they keeping up this medical side-show? They know I'm aware that this is a simulation. They could have done anything, put me anywhere...

But they think I don't know this is a simulation. This is for me. They're explaining the "physical" trauma from the recalibration to someone who isn't supposed to know what that is. Somehow or other, they don't know that we... well, that we're talking.

Night nodded (mentally speaking). *Then maybe they can't see everything after all. That gives us some wiggle-room. You want the center seat, Lieutenant?*

Only metaphorically. Stick close by, Number One.

Aye aye.

Slowly, Kovach opened his eyes. The old bear looked down, used a pen light to check his reactions. "PERRLA. Good sign. Assuming that your brain functioned in the first place, it's not gotten any worse for all this. Vitals slowing to baseline. Think it's time to get that stick out of your muzzle?"

The tiger nodded. Hazlitt took gentle hold of it. "Good. You look like a dog with a bone, and that's unbecoming in a feline of your stature. Just open slowly…"

Stick removed, Kovach tried to work his dry tongue around to form words, but it wasn't so easy. The bear nodded, reached to one side, and brought forth a cup with a straw. "Don't drown. It would be very ungrateful of you."

The doctor held the tiger's head up as he managed to suck some water from the cup. He pulled away to show he was finished, at least for now, and managed to squeak out, "Wha' happen'?"

"We don't know." The doctor sighed. "Got a med alert from your cabin; internal sensors picked up some kind of disturbance. EmTees found you in your recliner, passed out after what seemed to be a moderate seizure of some kind, brought you in here, and you had a whopper. I want to keep you here for a few days, make sure you're all right…"

Kovach blinked. Hazlitt had frozen in his position, not even breathing. Inside his mind, Night watched as Kovach – the body and the tiger inside his head – shuddered and grunted for a moment, like a recalibration but nowhere near as severe. The environment shifted, melted, changed. Night found himself in a hospital bed on the sick ward, perhaps where Tolliver had been some time before. The lighting was normal, the space clean, and the bear had shifted to the other side of the bed, a different-colored bow tie and shirt underneath the uniform lab coat. He looked down at Kovach, smiling.

"Well, good news, Kovach – you can finally quit whining about the chow they send down here to sick bay. I'm discharging you."

"So soon?"

"Four days isn't enough for you?"

Inside his mind, Kovach shook his head. He looked at Night. *Can you see this?*

I can see enough. Night felt more than actually saw it – memory fill-in for four days of being in sick bay, from tests to bad food, from boredom to short visits from Perryman and Baptiste, complete with innocuous dialog. The scenario had been accelerated to allow Kovach's "cloak" to process the passage of time. None of it would be consistent with the in-sim personality development that had given Kovach and the others something close to a mind of their own. The question was, how much of this fill-in had been given to the others? Would it overwrite their separate development? And where was Tolliver in all this?

"Did we ever pin down what it was, Doc?" Kovach asked.

The bear's brows knitted a bit. "Haven't been paying attention, eh, Kovach?"

The tiger recovered quickly. "We talked about so many possibilities, I kinda lost track of the final diagnosis."

"Simple as can be. Congenital. Minor wiring defect in the brain that was triggered by that fighting simulation you were in. Could have been triggered by damn near anything, just like a flashing light could trigger an epileptic seizure. Once we found it, we were able to patch you up with microsurgery." The doctor touched a slightly tender location somewhere behind Kovach's left ear. "Hardly see a thing even now. You'll even re-grow your fur the right color, before much longer."

"That's great, Doc." Kovach forced a smile. "I suppose you're going to tell me to take it easy for a few days more, right?"

"At least don't go hefting weights for hours liked that damned rabbit," Hazlitt grumped. "I've given strict instructions that you're not to go near anything that might over-stimulate your cerebral cortex for at least two more days, and I want..."

Again the bear froze. Both Night and Kovach seemed to expect it. Inside his mind, Night reached out quickly, held Kovach tightly as the tiger went through another session of trembling and grunts. The scene changed again, this time ending with Kovach sitting half-naked on an exam table as Hazlitt, turned from him, was putting some instruments away in a small cabinet near the bed. "All right, put your shirt back on, you're fine. I'm glad that they let you have that extra day off, though. I thought they'd want you back in that damned simulation almost immediately."

"They don't like to waste time, do they, Doc?" Kovach slipped back into his tunic shirt, trying to let himself absorb the information of everything that he did over what was now a week of programmed information. Night, immune from the direct programming, saw it as something around 11 minutes. Kovach shook his head, sorting it all out. At one point, he stopped and frowned. Night seemed to catch the image.

Who is that?

His name's Mueller. Works on the flight deck.

Handsome feller. Not sure I've ever made it with a Saluki before.

They're more durable than they look.

I didn't think I could get into that position...

You didn't. I did.

But even if you work out more than I do...

What part of "simulation" did you not understand?

"Kovach? Are you all right?"

"Woolgathering, Doc." He stood, shaking his head slightly. "I'm out of here."

"And about time too." Doc Hazlitt clapped him on the shoulder. "Don't take this the wrong way, tiger, but I don't want to see you in here again."

Kovach walked out of the sick bay, still a little confused by the sense of processing a week's worth of memories in what Night was able to confirm was actually a short time. He walked slowly, taking a more or less direct route to the mess, figuring it to be the best place to start. He might or might not be hungry, but it was better than going back to his cabin at the moment.

I'm not sure if that was unexpectedly nice of them, or if they have a voyeur in the audience.

I'd guess the latter, Night said in his mind. *And what was that tiny egg-looking thing you strapped onto his—*

Focus.

I don't think I've ever heard that kind of moaning from—

Not there, you idiot.

Yeah, okay. Right. So … what's our plan?

You're asking me? I'm just the flyboy program, you're the one playing God.

Night had nothing to say for a long moment. Kovach stopped walking, and in his mind, he took Night into his arms. *I had no right to say that. I'm sorry.*

In a way, I'm glad you did. For one thing, I needed to hear it. For another, it tells me that you've still got the independent streak that you gained from your separate experiences. It means that they haven't overwritten you, just added to you.

They don't see the rest of me, so to speak?

It's mountains of code; they can't possibly work through it all in such a short time. They're not likely to look too closely anyway. They want answers, and they want them yesterday.

And what about you? They have to know you're here, wearing this "cloak." Do you think they can hear us?

No; we'd have found that out by now. They'd have shut us down. I admit, I wish I knew how they jacked me in here.

How did they get your friend? Donovan?

Good news there – they didn't. Donovan speaks German fluently, it was his first language. I wondered about it when I realized that he hadn't said a word of German the whole time we were at the resort. When I spoke to him in German, he'd have answered in German, and he'd have known that what I said was, "What do you want? Living space?" Someone who couldn't tap a translation program fast enough took a guess at what I said and answered as best he could.

So they don't have him, in your world?

They may have him, but he's not jacked in. They tried to fake him, to manipulate me.

Then you don't have to cooperate. You can get out of here.

Not yet. They won't let me just walk out a door, even if I could find it. I'm going to have to bring this simulation to a halt.

Entering the mess, Kovach paused briefly. *Will that kill me?*

Night felt himself sigh softly. *I don't know. I have a backup of you on my redundant servers – at least as much of you as it could get before this whole thing went nuts. But I don't know if it's you. I'm a lousy excuse for a god, Kovach.*

It was Kovach's turn to be silent, even as he went through the motions of building dinner (based upon ship's time, it was only a little early for it), taking his tray to the cashier and waving his bright orange pin drive at the register (*at least they finally kept a color,* Night thought). He sat down at a table, took a few bites, and then it was his turn to sigh.

The condemned prisoner ate a hearty meal. Kovach considered, trying to reach some kind of understanding. *You gave me more knowledge and experience than you thought. This place... this simulation... for me, for us, it's become The Village. We have to escape, and it may be that we have to bring this place down to do it. If I have to die, let me do it as myself. Not a number... a free spirit.*

In the staging place, Night looked into Kovach's eyes. *Hokahey.*

19

"Mind if I join you?"

Kovach looked up from his meal and smiled warmly. "You're always welcome, Baptiste. Good to see you. Doing all right?"

"I should be asking you that." The Husky set her tray on the table and sat opposite the tiger. "All that time in sick bay… you must have bored your tail off."

"Nope, still got it." Kovach lashed his tail about as if to prove it. "It wasn't so bad. Time just seemed to fly by. And thanks for coming to visit, by the way."

"Least I could do. I figured I'd better time it so that Hazlitt was away when I came to visit. Tell me, does he really think he's got a chance with me?"

"Mostly wishful thinking, but yeah, the old bear definitely has you in his sights."

"Evasive Maneuver Pattern Delta!"

Kovach laughed. "He's not that bad. I'm just glad he allowed visitors." He paused. Night nodded his approval: *Keep testing.* The tiger forked another bite of food, then continued. "I should go thank Perryman as well. I'm glad you two came by. Sort of surprised that I didn't hear from Tolliver as well."

"I think he's just tired of sick bay himself," she chuckled. "He looks good. Good as new."

"Then everything's fine."

"Yep. Couldn't be better."

"Living the dream." Kovach let the conversation drop for a bit, as both pilots ate their food in a reflective silence. Night was anxious to see what else Baptiste might know, but he kept his muzzle shut, nodding again to Kovach. The pilot knew Baptiste better than he did.

Head down, as if talking to her food, Baptiste asked, "What did you and Perryman talk about?"

Kovach thought about it, trying to run through the implanted memories to see if there was anything important. "Nothing, really. It's true what they say: Visitors in hospital rarely talk about anything important, as if it's bad luck or something."

"I guess I kept things pretty simple too." Her tone seemed strained. "Not like we've got a lot of important things to talk about, I guess."

Baptiste looked up sharply, and Kovach felt his blood grow cold with what he saw in her eyes. *She knows,* he thought to Night, *or she suspects.*

I don't think we can tell her.

She's got a right—!

Yes, she does. But if they're screwing with simulation time, they may cut us short at any moment. A little truth may be worse than all of it. We don't know how much time we have before they get bored and stick us in the Phibriglex-62 sim.

I'm going to try something. Stay with me.

"It's okay, Baptiste. I think you're important. So is Perryman. We can't just throw in the towel and pretend we don't see what we see."

Something in the Husky's eyes flickered. She stared at Kovach, who nodded his head about a millimeter in response. "True," she said. "I just feel like we've gone through so much so quickly."

"I know exactly what you mean," Kovach said softly. "It's difficult to keep track of things, sometimes. You wonder if you can trust your own judgment. Don't worry too much. Whatever happens, I'll believe in you, if you'll believe in me."

The tiger reached across the table to Baptiste and took one of her forepaws in hers. Quickly, he pressed his fingers into her paw, using the pilot's code signs: *Message received.* She signaled back to him: *Verified.* "I've always believed in you, tiger, even when you're being a pompous hotshot." She smiled to take the sting out of the epithet.

"I'd follow you anywhere, ya know," Kovach replied. "Except to bed."

"Your loss," she smiled at him. She signaled to him: *Escape plan?* He signaled back: *Yes. Code follows.*

"I should go visit Perryman before turning in."

"Not like you'll have much more luck there," the Husky joked.

"True, but maybe I can get him to watch a video with me. He's got built-in 3-D goggles."

"Ew!" Baptiste wrinkled her nose. "That seemed a bit harsh."

"Didn't mean it to be; sorry. He'd probably forgive me if I offered him a bottle of good ale."

"Just trying to get him drunk."

"Whatever works." With a final gentle squeeze, Kovach released her paw and stood. "And hey, if I don't get him, more for you... unless you're saving yourself for Doc Hazlitt."

"Bite your tongue." Baptiste smiled. "Get some rest. I have the feeling we may be working hard in the morning."

The pilots left the mess and walked to the main corridor, where they shared a friendly hug. His muzzle actually touching her ear, Kovach whispered, "I need you to trust me."

"Completely."

They separated and walked in opposite directions.

* * * * *

Kovach found Perryman at rest, which made his cabin a bit more neutrally scented. The rabbit was glad to see his fellow pilot, although he was also agitated in a way that Kovach hadn't seen before. "Thanks for coming to visit me in hospital," the tiger began. "It really helped the time pass."

"You're welcome." Perryman's eye darted around the room, coming to rest on Kovach's face, accompanied by a small, tight frown. "Had to make sure you were going to return to work. Gotta watch you slackers."

The tiger shook his head minutely. "Yeah, like I'm gonna let you handle that whole simulation by yourself, huh? Don't believe it. I'm gonna see it through."

"You think they've got the bugs worked out of it?"

"Oh, I suspect they've had someone working on the problem since it first happened. These guys don't want to wait; they expect us to be ready for anything."

"So it would seem."

A ping sounded from the rabbit's computer console. He padded to the table to look at the alert, nodding. "You'll be getting one of those too, I'm pretty sure. Confirmation for Phibriglex-62 sim. Not too early in the day, but we'd all be better off getting some sleep." He looked over his shoulder. "I'd better shut down the console; don't need some idiot sending me spam in the middle of the night, setting off some damned alarm."

"Good plan. And you won't get much sleep if I stay here." Kovach watched Perryman execute a series of shut-down commands on his main console, then do the same to his tablet. "You'll huddle in a corner, expecting me to jump your bones."

"You're saying you wouldn't?"

"Only with your permission. I hate having to chase down my prey."

"Fair enough. Listen, Kovach, I'm glad you came by. I'll see you out." The rabbit motioned for the tiger to stay where he stood, and came up close enough to grip him by the shoulders. His muzzle not two millimeters from Kovach's ear, Perryman whispered, "Don't get any ideas. This is in case we're still being monitored. They're expecting to hear the door open, so we've got about fifteen seconds."

Kovach nodded quickly, refraining from making the joke about rabbits being quick.

Perryman continued, "Someone is screwing with our heads. It's as if time has been condensed, or memories altered."

"What's your clue?"

"I have memories, including visual memories, but only with my real eye; the Oculus has no record whatsoever. Even its time-synch is off."

YES! In Kovach's mind, Night punched the air. *I'll explain later.*

"Someone's playing a bad game."

"Yes," Kovach whispered into the rabbit's ear. "Bigger than I can explain. They can't see everything. I've got answers, but they're a bitch to tell quickly. Will you trust me?"

"You've got some help. I can 'see' it."

Night felt himself quiver slightly; Kovach whispered, "Can you see him?"

"The cyber... not clear, but something..."

"Perryman – I need your help."

In the otherwise quiet room, Perryman's breath sounded loud in Kovach's ear. "Are you in danger?"

"All of us are. But there may be a way out. Will you trust me?"

After a long moment, the rabbit pulled slightly away from the tiger and looked at him with his real eye. Then he bent forward and planted a lingering kiss on Kovach's lips. He pulled back, a faint smile playing on his muzzle in response to the tiger's look of stunned surprise. "Just in case that's my last chance to do that. Now... go get some sleep."

20

"Snake Lady Simulation, Phibriglex-62, launch in three, two, one…"

Kovach closed his eyes, and inside his head, he wrapped both arms around Night and thought, *Hold on to your stomach!*

The launch simulation was as breakfast-unfriendly as ever; Kovach's body had at least some expectation, whereas Night felt as if he were being shot out through a scale-model bazooka. Several words were expressed through thought, in rapid and particularly obscene succession.

Couldn't have said it better myself, Kovach observed.

You could have if I hadn't made the game PG-rated!

After several seconds, Kovach released Night and opened his body's eyes. Despite the dire situation and the loose bits of radio traffic in Kovach's ears, Night still had to appreciate the intricacy and beauty of the simulation. He would almost certainly never experience star travel in his real life; this was as close as he would get. As if looking over Kovach's shoulder, he observed the panorama through the viewport as well as the various instruments and readouts, trying to absorb it all with the same ease and experience that Kovach had acquired. The programming – some little part of it his own – was exquisite. There really was little reason to think that this wasn't real.

It's incredible, he thought.

Kovach considered. *I feel almost as though I've grown up with it. Dreaming of star travel since I was a kit; worked hard, took the tests, got through the training, made it out here. Flying like this… it's been my life.* He paused. *Night, for what it's worth… thank you.*

Night put a paw on the pilot's shoulder. *Not over yet.*

Phibriglex-62 unfolded in its own time, Sarge keeping things active, as was his job. The first encounter was reasonably tame; Night could see in Kovach's mind that it was close enough to the first run-through that it made no odds. *It's déjà vu all over again,* he thought.

Funny, genius. Kovach sighed. For all practical purposes, the two of them had talked through the night, Kovach's body seeming to be dozing, or tossing a bit from time to time. Night had experienced many a night of restless thoughts, but he'd never before had the sensation of actually talking in whole sentences, and getting replies that sometimes surprised him. In the end, a plan had been forged, and although he wasn't necessarily happy about it, Night was reasonably optimistic. Kovach had the technical skill necessary to work the simulation; all Night had to do was to create some kind of active code, mentally, on the fly, to compromise a simulation within a simulation, to make sure that his work went unrecorded if not unobserved, and ultimately to destroy himself without dying.

A day in the life of a geek. Hardly even exciting.

The second encounter was a bit more interesting, but no one had broken out the big guns for it. Group leader Lentz ordered Baptiste and Kovach to intercept an unusual-looking vehicle that more resembled an egg-colored sphere than anything else. It seemed to have something wrong with its shielding, because to the naked eye, it seemed to wobble and bounce slightly as it hung otherwise unmoving in space.

Through the headset, Kovach heard, "Hailing starcraft, this is Lieutenant Baptiste of the galactic cruiser *Heartwielder.* Please respond."

A soft, mellifluous voice replied, "We do not know of *Heartwielder.* What are your intentions?"

"Our intentions are peaceful. *Heartwielder* is not a military or war-based ship. I am part of a small, purely defensive force. We have been sent only to contact you. What are your intentions?"

"We are an exploratory group, at this time seeking to make contact with one of our own who has been lost. We are non-aggressive and wish only to find our mutual friend."

Inside Kovach's mind, Night's ears pricked up sharply.

"Do you wish assistance? We can relay your information back to *Heartwielder,* to see if we can provide help."

"We thank you. At this time, we ask only that you let us be on our way. We have hope of making contact on our own. If we may contact you later, we would be grateful of your assistance then."

"May we ask for a name for your vessel, so that others may recognize your call signal?"

"Rover."

Kovach blinked as he felt Night punch the air.

"Please allow us to send information to you, as background for our next encounter."

"Acknowledged, Rover; standing by."

Kovach checked his instruments, his onboard computers acknowledging and accepting the data stream from the strangely ball-like ship. The systems confirmed no malicious software or intent; information arrived in neatly identified packets and in formats that could be easily filed and accessed at a later time.

Did Baptiste get it too? Night thought urgently.

Yes; in fact, it's probably being passed along to the other ships in the simulation. Is it dangerous?

Not to us. Can you get Batiste on a private comm channel?

Yes. You want to talk?

Yes, but I can't fly at the same time. Relay what I tell you. Please, he added politely.

Kovach smirked. *Good manners will out.*

Baptiste thanked Rover for the information, reported back to Lentz and the rest of Snake Lady, then clicked over to answer Kovach's call. "You okay?"

"Fine." Kovach listened quickly to Night's words and repeated them. "Copy that signal into your tablet. Do you have it with you?"

"Yes. Perryman told me to bring it; he has his too. What's this about?"

"I need you to trust me. Tell Perryman to copy over his data, to the tablet or to his cyber-eye, either one. Remember me telling you I've got help? There's a message in there. I'll tell you how to find it later. Back to main channel."

"Switching."

Kovach and Baptiste's craft settled back into Snake Lady's formation as the Sarge's voice came over the main intercom. "Nice of you two to join us. Everybody nice and level; we'll give you guys a minute or two to relax."

What the hell is Rover?

Takes a while to explain. Quick, transfer that signal into your pad. Bring up folder contents, or table of contents, file names, whatever you got.

Okay, okay, don't rush me … there. What are we looking for?

Through Kovach's eyes, Night scanned the list. *That one! Open up the one called Village.*

Kovach tried to open it. *Encrypted. Got a password?*

Try "You are Number Six."

The tiger entered the phrase. After a moment, the screen changed to reveal a second challenge question: WHO ARE YOU?

Now what?

Night thought furiously. He considered the source, knew that it wouldn't be difficult, but that it also had to be something no one else would think of. What was it he had been told…? The answer broke like dawn.

"Schizoid Man."

Kovach entered the words. The screen dissolved into a picture of a screaming face pressed outward from inside a broad, thin layer of something like rubber or latex, then of a huge wobbling spheroid of rubber bounding down a deserted beach. A third challenge: WHAT HAPPENED?

Night didn't even hesitate. *"Rover got him."*

Kovach typed. *Please allow me this opportunity to reiterate… you're weird.*

The screen dissolved again, finally replaced with a complex code set, and the following short note: *Night – this is the best we could come up with, based on your descriptions. Good luck. Gemini.*

The best what?

The best way out.

Care to share with the rest of the class?

They couldn't just repeat the first Phibriglex-62 sim; everyone would be ready for that. They had to put in something else in the middle. Gemini couldn't hack in directly, but he left a message inside a relatively harmless confrontation simulation, hoping they'd put in some fluff before the real exercise. I know that part of the sim came from him – he stuck that ship in there with just enough references to The Prisoner *to alert me when we found it. What he sent may be enough code for me to work with.*

To do what?

To give them what they want. Except they won't get it. I'm going to –

"Okay, folks, let's get back to work." Sarge's voice cut through the headset. "Cream puff time is over; let's see if you can make this one work."

A distant contact flicker on one of Kovach's panels triggered a need to report. *Do it,* Night said in his head. *Make it seem normal.*

"Snake Lady, Medusa Six, contact aft, 165 relative, speed point-two, configuration not recognized. Verify."

"Medusa Four," said Rains, the white tiger's perfect Londoner's accent not showing the slightest stress. "Contact confirmed; clueless here, mates."

"Medusa One," Lentz identified, "Rains, Tolliver, go have a look; the rest of us, sit tight and hold formation. We'll be listening in, guys."

Kovach watched two of the Starhawks break and head toward the potential intruder. *Couldn't be better,* Night chuckled nervously in Kovach's head. *Two allies and the top cat.*

What are you —

Don't worry, we won't hurt him. That's not what plasma shurikens do, after all.

Kovach felt a chill rock through him that was painfully close to the sensation of recalibration. Inside is mind, he felt Night step up to him and hold him tightly. Both experienced the physical sensations of shaking, of adrenaline kicking into high gear, of knowing something that was supposed to be beyond knowing – a moment signaling the passing of a point of no return.

We can do this. We'll get through this. It's going to take us both. Ready?

Oh hells no. But we'll do it anyway.

Night grinned, a rictus of precisely one half exhilaration, one half terror. *Fasten your seat belts, everybody... it's gonna be a bumpy ride.*

21

I need the tablet, Night thought, *and you need to keep piloting. So I'm going to try something a little weird.*

What Kovach felt was similar to putting one's arm through the sleeve of a long-sleeved shirt, except that his arm was the sleeve, and the sensation went all the way down to his forepaw. As Kovach watched his own paw make notes and check information on his data pad, he tried to keep at least some attention on what was going on with the rest of the Snake Lady crew. Tolliver and Rains were making contact with the new target, and the conversation seemed quite banal. On the tablet, a new window was asking for identification.

Phase One, Night thought. He entered the username NUMBER TWO and the password HAMMER INTO ANVIL. The information passed through whatever systems it needed to and came back with a screen filled with information, with the header of PHIBRIGLEX-62.

How did you do that?

First rule of programming, Kovach: Always leave yourself a back door to crawl through.

Kovach's paw continued to dance across the tablet. The tiger felt himself envious of the speed and complexity of the operation. Then again, he went to flight school, getting some damned fine scores; the brass was... He broke off the thought, realizing that it was all only programming. No memories, no history, no self. He was only bits and bytes in the very same program that Night was manipulating, and the paw that was doing the work was less than a ghost in the machine until someone put it on, like a cloak, or a glove...

Kovach? Night's voice in his head interrupted him.

Yeah, I'm here.

A pause. *I think it's ready.*

The tiger nodded. If nothing else, he realized, his programming had at least given him the tenacity and raw guts to see it through.

Okay, genius. What was that war cry you said?

Hokahey. In movies, it means, "It's a good day to die." It really means something more like, "Let's do it," but the other interpretation is so much more butch.

Kovach managed a smirk. *I don't think either of us would fail a testosterone test at this point.*

Outside the Starhawk, an infinity of stars glowed in an ocean of blackness; beyond that, somewhere that Kovach would never know, was a place where one could have a real day, to experience a real death. He took a long, deep breath, then exhaled sharply, experiencing what he could of his body while he still had at least the simulation of one.

"Hokahey," he said softly.

"Not understood, Medusa Six, repeat message."

Ready, flyboy?

Let's do it, genius.

Phase Two. Kovach's paw moved across the pad, activating a set of instructions. The tablet glowed with the words DEGREE ABSOLUTE.

"Medusa Six, repeat message."

Kovach felt Night release his paw. In his mind, he felt Night hug him tightly. Illusion, all illusion… yet there was something else, something that couldn't be faked. The one thing in the universe that was a constant, that could be experienced and never truly taken away. What he experienced was love.

Phase Three?

On it, boss.

Kovach opened is muzzle and shouted: "HOKAHEY!"

Medusa Six broke formation and sped through space back toward *Heartwielder.* Chatter in his headphones provided nothing the least bit surprising. Sarge flung curses and epithets, Lentz tried to restore order, and somewhere out there, Tolliver and Rains were breaking off dealing with the unknown ship. Kovach ignored them all and put Perryman and Baptiste on a private channel.

"If Lentz tells you to bring me down with shurikens, tell him they're offline."

"Copy," came two swift replies. Kovach felt his heart squeeze with genuine happiness. His friends were real.

"Medusa Six," Lentz shouted into his mike, "return to formation or be disabled."

Grinning insanely, Kovach answered, "Hey, pinhead, I just heard a joke about your sister, wanna hear it?"

"Medusa Three, disable."

"Shurikens offline."

"Medusa Five, disable."

"Shurikens offline. He must have done something to them!" Baptiste upped the ante.

Nice one, puppy! Kovach thought. Night chuckled and made a thumbs-up motion.

Lentz's ship accelerated and began to execute an attack pass. Kovach nodded; Lentz knew that Tolliver and Rains were too far away to make the run.

Make it easy for him.

You sure about this?

That's why they call it Degree Absolute.

Gee, thanks.

"Engaging shurikens," Lentz announced. Enemy combatants wouldn't hear the exchange, and it was clear that Lentz didn't give a damn if Kovach heard it either. Starhawk training was as ingrained as breathing. "Kovach, break off. Do it now."

"You know you won't kill me with those things."

"You don't want to know what I'll do to you when you get back aboard ship!"

"Oh go on, surprise me."

"Target acquired," Lentz said, clearly finished with conversation. "Launching shurikens."

A small, bright torpedo-like bolt launched from a tube on the undercarriage of Medusa One, aiming directly for the engines of Medusa Six. In a sort of idiotic reflexive move, both Night and Kovach counted the seconds... *three... two... one...*

Medusa Six was encompassed in a blinding flash of pyrotechnics, rocking and shuddering through the impact of the plasma shuriken. From outside, it would have appeared as if the ship had been vaporized inside the cloud of vivid flames, an explosion worthy of the most destructive weapons available. From inside, Kovach held himself still and stiff waiting for the conflagration and violence to end. What surprised him was that it didn't even start in the first place.

In Kovach's mind, Night crowed with triumph. *It's all a fake! They don't know how to make a plasma shuriken work! That's what they needed me for! All they could do was make fireworks but not blow up the ship – paradox.* The programmer slapped the pilot excitedly on his back. *Now we can push forward.*

You're sure they won't read your code?

We locked them out of the Phibriglex simulation as soon as we executed Degree Absolute. Everything we do in here is invisible to them.

Then why don't they shut down the whole simulation, Heartwielder and all?

They can't. If they try, they'll get an error message telling them that they can't shut down while Phibriglex is running. If they pull the plug on everything without reconciling that, they lose everything. Literally.

Medusa Six flew out of the smoke and flames completely intact and fully functioning, much to the great shock of everyone concerned. Kovach stitched the ship through the short distance between himself and Medusa One. "Okay, Lentz," he said with more calm than he felt. "Let me show you what a real plasma shuriken does."

From below the Starhawk flew a small burst of light that looked like a flat, multi-pointed object tumbling end over end toward the other small ship. It struck directly on the hull plating at Medusa One's engine mounting and passed into it without seeming to have hit the ship at all. A moment later, every light on the ship flashed brightly then went out completely. The Starhawk was powerless and adrift in space.

"Much quieter, don't you agree, Lentz? Oh, wait, you can't hear me, can you? Rains, Tolliver, you might want to go get Medusa One; he's got oxygen for a while, but he'll need help getting back to *Heartwielder*. We'll see you there."

On the private channel, Perryman spoke up. "I've never seen anything like it."

"You've never seen a plasma shuriken."

"But we've used them in the past!" Baptiste cried.

"We've been lied to, pup. And we're about to fix that. Follow me back to *Heartwielder*. We're going to finish this off together, and then I'm going to buy us drinks and tell you a story you won't believe."

Am I lying to them? he asked Night.

Not if I can help it, Kovach. The pilot felt a paw on his shoulder, there in the cockpit, and he was as reassured as he was going to be.

On the main channel Sarge was trying regain control of his mutinying crew. "Kovach, I'll have your tail cut off for this!"

"Never knew you were so attracted to it, Sarge. I could have one made for you." On the private channel, he continued. "We're going to bring the engines down without knocking out the life support. We'll need surgical strikes. I'm sending coordinates."

"Why aren't they shutting down Phibriglex?"

"They're locked out of the system. They can't shut anything down until we end the simulation ourselves."

"And no one is coming to our cubicles to yank us bodily out of the simulation pods, are they?"

Baptiste's question hung in the silent void as both Kovach and Night searched for an answer.

"Kovach," Perryman breathed softly. "It's not what we thought, is it?"

Baptiste added, "*We're* not what we thought."

After a long silence, Perryman spoke up again. "Baptiste and I talked about it. We don't have the answers, but we think that maybe we... figured something out."

Kovach's voice caught in his throat. "I wish we had time for me to tell you everything. All I can say is that this is the way out, if you receive my meaning."

There was a chuckle in Perryman's voice when he said, "Fancy talk for a pilot. You really must have someone in there with you."

"Any idea what will happen?" the Husky asked.

"Not a clue. Just a hope. And maybe that's all anyone has." In his mind, Kovach looked at Night. *Want to tell them anything?*

Yes... but there's no time. Night felt tears forming, fought them back. *Doubt you can fly too well with me bawling my head off like a kit. Let's do this.*

Hokahey. Kovach nodded. "Perryman... Baptiste... you know what to do." He paused. "I don't know if this matters, but I'm going to say it anyway. I love you both."

"Now you tell me," Perryman laughed.

"Guess I'll have to pick another way to show you how much fun females can be." Baptiste's voice cracked a little. "Let's do it."

"This time," Kovach grinned, "I'll say yes."

Three Starhawks took their simulation home.

22

"How do we play it, Kovach?"

"Tight and fast. They may try to jam our communications; if they do, take whatever action you think best, don't wait to figure out what the rest of us are doing. They probably have already figured out that their plasma shurikens don't work, so they're going to break out the real stuff. Our shields are strong, we're good fliers, and if we're lucky, we should be able to take our shots from a distance."

"Our shurikens will work?" Baptiste sounded slightly less than confident.

"We own it. They're not going to try to disable us. This one's for real."

Perryman laughed. "In a manner of speaking."

Night felt another twinge of guilt, but Kovach snorted. "Okay, two minutes to *Heartwielder*."

"Why don't they scramble a squad of Starhawks?" the Husky wondered.

"The Phibriglex sim was created like a training mission for a single squad; they never created a scenario where they'd need backup."

"Then why would *Heartwielder* be powering its weapons? Is it even in the simulation?"

"We launched from there. Tell me you haven't forgotten those launches."

"Of course not… but after that, why would *Heartwielder* be involved in the rest of the simulation?"

Kovach felt a sinking in his stomach. It was only in that moment that he realized: None of them had ever run Phibriglex to its conclusion. Would the ship even be there? It wouldn't have to be there, for them to run battle simulations…

If you have to learn to launch, Night spoke up, *you have to learn to land, don't you?*

"We've never run a complete simulation of Phibriglex," Kovach said aloud, "but there has to be a simulation for returning the Starhawks to the ship. Haven't we made landings before?"

The silence in the headsets was not encouraging.

"Heartwielder in one minute." Kovach tried to sound reassuring.

"I hate to break this to you, tiger," Perryman said quietly, "but shouldn't we be seeing lights by now? Unless, of course they shut them all down."

"Or if it isn't really there." Baptiste didn't sound certain of anything anymore.

Think! Night screamed to himself. *There's an answer, there's got to be an answer!*

"Thirty seconds." Kovach licked his lips, tried to keep his tail still. He looked out the windows of his craft, able to see lights on the other two Starhawks. It was a simulation, of course, but the internal logic of the simulation remained intact. After breaking formation, Medusa Six changed course back to *Heartwielder,* a simple command to go back to the ship, essentially reversing the original flight instructions. Could the command be wrong? Kovach checked his instruments, feeling Night looking over his shoulder. Everything looked right, except that the main ship was nowhere in the vicinity.

"All stop," Kovach said without much conviction. In his windows, the other two Starhawks seemed to hang in space in front of him. "Any contacts, either of you?"

"Negative" and "Nope" sounded in his ears.

"Baptiste, coordinates?" The Husky rattled off her numbers. "Perryman?" He produced his own numbers, and no one had to tell anyone else that they weren't even close. "I'd give you mine, but you've already guessed."

"If these numbers are correct, we're half a hundred thousand klicks away from each other." Perryman's voice revealed the frown that must have been on his face. "Either of you have any information on the other Starhawks?"

"Completely off my grids," Baptiste reported. "I hate to use a cliché, but it's as if we're in uncharted space."

Echoing Night's thoughts, Kovach said aloud, "We've pushed outside of the boundaries of the simulation."

"...oh gods..." Baptiste's voice was small in Kovach's headphones, but he didn't need to ask what the problem was; he could see it as easily as the others. Night ground his teeth (or performed its equivalent) because he had seen this sort of thing before. Kovach simply stared, borrowing his understanding from Night directly.

Across the screens, the starfield simulation remained perfect, up to a point. Just beyond what passed for "local space" was a flickering, stuttering collection of pixilated images, not-quite stars, false nebulae, and a seemingly infinite collection of fluorescing green lines like ley lines on a map, waiting for the cartographer to finish his job and create the rest of the universe. They had reached the edges of the simulation; there wasn't even a solid reference point to go back to. No one had bothered to write the program this far.

Silence expressed their combined thoughts better than words; no one had the slightest idea what to do. Inside Kovach's mind, even Night seemed confounded and at a loss. Everything depended upon ending the *Heartwielder* simulation, and the only way to attack it without being shut down was to hijack the Phibriglex sim and attack from within. With Phibriglex effectively frozen, there was nothing for anyone to do but...

Night said something that would have changed the rating of the game.

Do I want to know? Kovach asked quietly.

Probably not, but we can't do it without the others' help. I'll tell you; you explain it to them.

"Stand by," Kovach said, then fell silent, absorbing the information from Night. After about thirty seconds, Kovach repeated what Night first said.

Perryman spoke up, "I swear I didn't know you could say something like that."

"I probably can't; I'm just imitating a friend of mine." He sighed deeply. "Okay. I have no idea if this is going to work, but it's about our only shot at this point. I'm really pushing the limits of trust here."

"Between following you and doing nothing," Baptiste said, "you're a better bet. Fill us in, tiger."

He did. Both Perryman and Baptiste imitated Kovach's friend, then fell silent.

"Any better ideas?"

"Lots… but they all involve being anywhere but here."

"So… we take the shot?"

Baptiste blew out her breath forcefully. "Guess ya gotta die from something."

"Let's hope for a better outcome than that," Perryman said. "This is really gonna screw with my cyber, isn't it?"

Kovach listened, then repeated Night's words. "No idea, honestly. You'll have to tell us when we get there." He paused. "I'm beaming hard code to your pins; mine is configured the same way."

"You realize," the rabbit offered, "that this all depends upon exactly when and where Phibriglex actually begins?"

"Yup."

"Are we going to know what we're doing?"

"I doubt it. But that's planned in. As much as it can be."

Baptiste snorted a bitter laugh. "Not much different from now. Hey, Kovach? Whoever your friend is, tell him…" She paused. "Tell him, thanks for the laughs. And for a good friend."

"Make that for two," Perryman added.

"Done and done," Kovach said. To Night, he said, *If this doesn't work, what happens to you?*

I'll probably be stuck in a simulation somewhere until my body rots, and then who in hell knows?

Yeah… speaking of Hell…

"Here goes." Kovach settled himself back in his cockpit chair and tried to relax himself as much as possible. In the silent farewells in the headsets, the tiger gave himself one last full breath and spoke.

"Reboot."

And everything stopped.

* * * * *

Utter blackness. Utter silence. Night had some vague semblance of awareness, something more than being asleep yet less than being unconscious. He had the insane sensation of being reassembled somehow, as if his mind were looking for ways to connect itself to the rest of him. A few wisps of sound came to his ears, a faint hiss of sound, something beeping, and a whiff of something… familiar, very familiar, comforting, pungent, well-remembered… He wanted to speak, but he couldn't quite remember how to do that, as if something were disconnected…

"Sound off, Snake Lady. Medusa One…"

Roll call. Six pilots: Lentz, Tolliver, Perryman, Rains, Baptiste, Kovach.

"Well damned if they didn't get themselves in the right order," the bulldog grumbled, cocking his chin toward a door in the bulkhead that sighed open as he spoke. "Designation's on each chamber. Pick the right door, set up, jack in, you know the routine. SimRun designation Phibriglex-62. We'll boot you up. Get moving before I boot yer tails."

The chambers were in designation order; Kovach took up the one nearest the bulkhead door. The pilot's chair faced him as he entered. He spun, sat in the chair, found the initial controls as he settled his tail into position and pivoted the chair back toward the main console and viewport. Detaching the bright orange personal pin drive from the lanyard around his neck, he jacked into the primary data 'corder, ready to record his every move. His fore and hind paws moved automatically, checking sensors, touch-plates, joysticks and other controllers. Lights and screens came up at his command; the boards hummed with power, pinging and chiming with soft positive acknowledgements as the full power of the control systems came online…

For a split second, everything froze in place. Kovach became aware of someone else, someone… in his head? He shivered as information came pouring into place. The data pad in front of him bore the flashing letters DEGREE ABSOLUTE. Transfer complete, Kovach began to move again, connecting to a private channel. "Perryman? Baptiste?"

"Yo."

"Confirmed."

On the public channel, Sarge's voice could be heard loudly. "Okay, pups, kits, and others, get ready for synch. Systems up."

Privately, Kovach issued the command. "Ready shurikens."

"Online."

"Lock'n'load."

Sarge continued, not hearing what was going on right under his snout. "We've got a nice set of chain yankin' ready for you, starting with simulated launch. Hope you didn't have anything slimy for breakfast, or you're likely to see it again."

Kovach! Shouted Night's voice in the pilot's head. *What are you waiting for?*

Aren't we supposed to wait for a dramatic pause or something?

LAUNCH THE DAMNED THINGS!

On the public channel, Kovach said, "Nothing personal, Sarge."

As if he'd heard nothing, Sarge went on: "Snake Lady Simulation, Phibriglex-62, launch in three..."

"Medusa Three, Medusa Five..."

"...two..."

"FIRE."

Six plasma shurikens tore through plating and distance as if they were nothing at all. Outside the sim-pods, through hallways, Jeffries tubes, bulkheads, sections of the ship that might or might not have existed, all in order to find their targets, brightly pulsing bees burned through their own reality to sting the most sensitive parts of the body electric. In seconds, they reached their multiple objectives, shed their shells, and triggered their electromagnetic pulses. Kovach had just enough time to note that readouts could not reconcile the information being sent to them before everything – including his own mind – went black.

23

Utter blackness. Utter silence. Night had some vague semblance of awareness, something more than being asleep yet less than being unconscious. He had the insane sensation of being reassembled somehow, as if his mind were looking for ways to connect itself to the rest of him. A few wisps of sound came to his ears, a faint hiss of sound, something beeping, and a whiff of something... familiar, very familiar, comforting, pungent, well-remembered... He wanted to speak, but he couldn't quite remember how to do that, as if something were disconnected...

A voice. He heard a voice. A steady, clear, familiar voice. *Listening more intently, I heard in reality a murmuring of voices. But my weakness prevented me from understanding what the voices said. Yet it was language, I was sure... Night?*

The tiger tried to move, tried to understand what was happening. He tried to take in deeper breaths, to get more oxygen, to clear his head. The scent returned to him, that familiar, pungent, comforting, deeply personal scent. He tried to speak, he knew that he could speak, if he could just remember just how it was done, how to open his lips, move his tongue, move his paw, if he could move his paw a little, because there was something he had to do...

"Mitternachtstiger? Can you hear me?"

A word, or rather a name. He focused on it, tried to say it, tried to communicate the word, to ask for his help before it was too late and they dragged him down again... *Donovan...* say the name, say *Donovan...*

"DOCTOR!" cried the voice. "SOMEBODY, QUICKLY!"

He tried to move himself, a paw, a finger, the tip of his tail, his head, anything. He had the feeling of being reassembled, of making connections again, this is my eyelid, this is my finger, this is my toe, this is my ear, this is my tail, this is my jaw, yes, that's the one, make the jaw work... Sensation – feeling, connection, feeling reconnected to things, my paw, yes, someone is holding my paw, someone is leaning close to me, and I know that scent, I know that hyena's scent, Donovan, it's you, touching my head, yes, good start, my head, with the connections, the monitor, tell him, tell him now...

"DOCTOR!"

Something pulled at him, pulled at his mind, telling him to relax, to let go, not to fight, it's cold out there, it's dangerous out there, come back home, come back to your friends, you know they miss you there...

Heavily padding pawsteps, voices, familiar voices, Donovan talking, squeezing his forepaw, squeeze back, send the signal... no, not a signal, he's not a pilot, I'm not a pilot, that's a game, it's just a game, this is not a game, not a game...

His eyelid pulled back. Light. Hurt. Bright light. Blink. Something rubbing up the base of his hindpaw.

"Negative Babinski."

"Good sign," drawled another familiar voice.

Close to his ear: "*Mitternachtstiger...* please, Night, wake up... please come back to me... *kannst du mich hören?*"

Let go, oozed a voice somewhere in his mind. *Come back to where it's safe, where you can learn and explore, and vacation in beautiful tropical sands… bring the hyena with you, he'll like it there, and we've got lots of other companions for you to play with, a really physically active Saluki who can bend in so many incredible ways, and who misses you, he misses you so very much, you wouldn't want to hurt him now would you, oh yes, we take care of our own, and you're ours, after all, you're ours, completely ours, you've always been ours…*

A squeeze on his paw. Code? Was there a code? Was he being watched? The pilots would know; he could trust them, they would know…

Somewhere in his groggy mind, he saw something like himself, a tiger, about the same size, strong, self-assured, powerful, his long dark-chestnut colored mane of headfur completely against regulations, but no one was going to kick him out of this fur's Starhawk squad for it, he was that good, and he damn well knew it. *Don't take this the wrong way, buddy,* he grinned at Night, *but I think you need this. Get outta here.*

The tiger reached back and fetched a slap that literally shook Night's eyes open. He grunted harshly, still not quite able to speak.

"Night!" Donovan cried. He positioned his head where the tiger could see it. "Night, you're back!"

"Donovan, get out of my way, or there'll be hyena sandwiches for lunch." The drawling voice appeared over Night's head. The large brown bear looked down and flashed a pen light at his eyes.

Hazlitt?

"PERRLA," the bear said. "Vitals rising, EEG reactive…"

Night felt himself more able to move, his jaw shifting, his forepaw trying to grip Donovan's, his mind fighting to work properly. He grunted, made some attempt at making noise, his throat was so dry, his tongue thick and immovable. "Wrrr..." he tried.

Donovan was petting his headfur, put his muzzle close to his ear. "I'm here, babe, I'm listening. Try again."

"Wyyyyrz..."

Night tried moving his free paw upward, saw Hazlitt trying to take it into his own paws, rubbing the tiger's paw briskly. "That's it, boy, fight your way upward, you can do it. Push through."

The tiger tried to move, shift his body, anything to make himself wake up. He shook both paws, trying to get them free of his well-intentioned captors. *Come back,* something whispered in him, *come back down...* and the figure of another tiger, one that looked a lot like him, that *felt* a lot like him, ran into the foggy voices in his brain and began to tear them apart with his bared claws. *Fight it!* the tiger screamed. *Fight it! Say the word!*

"Why... Whyz..." Night pushed as hard as he could against everything and everyone.

"He's seizing!"

"NO!" Night managed. The arms around him, to hold him down, retreated. "Whys... whyrs..." He breathed deeply, his thick dry tongue trying to move against dry mouth, dry teeth, dry throat, and with all his strength he shouted. *"WIRES!"*

No sound or movement from around him. Sluggishly, he made his head turn to see Donovan, a confused look on his face, and he tried again. "WIRES," he said, the word harsh, hoarse, sandy dry. "NO... WIRES... PULL... WIRES..."

With more strength now, his forepaw moved toward his head. He could feel them now, the web of EEG wires on his head, sending its signals to the machine next to his bed. Night's eyes cut back and forth, looking frantically to Donovan, to Hazlitt, his body moving but without direct purpose, not quite able to obey his mind even now.

The bear glanced at the EEG monitor, leaned over to the head of the bed, and grabbed the bundle of wires at their junction. "Hold tight, tiger, this ain't fun."

Night croaked out once as Hazlitt yanked the wires harshly, tearing them from their connection points in a single hard pull. The bear put the wires to one side, then moved to help Donovan get Night into a sitting position, rearranging the oxygen cannula with its tiny pair of openings tucked carefully into Night's nostrils. The tiger panted heavily as he began to feel his body more fully again.

"Use your nose to inhale, Night; you need the oxygen." Hazlitt looked over the tiger's vital signs being reported from the finger monitor on his right forepaw. "These numbers are starting to look normal for a change. Can't say I'm unhappy about that, although I expect you to start complaining any minute now. You're probably dry as a bone; here, have a sip of water, and I mean just a sip."

Donovan held the cup and put the straw into Night's muzzle. Despite the urge to guzzle it down, he forced himself to take a sip and hold it in his mouth, trying to loosen up his tongue. After two more sips, he released the straw, still panting. Hazlitt had raised the upper portion of the bed, and Night fell back into a sitting position.

"P'lice," he said.

"What?"

His lips felt dry, caked, cracked. He tried to lick them, his rough feline tongue barely damp enough to help. "Get... p'lice. Will ex... plain."

The old bear looked at him steadily. "Are you really here, or still unconscious?"

Night blinked, tried to get his eyes to focus on the doctor. "How many... leads...?"

Hazlitt's eyebrows attempted to merge into one another. "Standard is 21. That's what the webbing is for."

"Check... leads." Night turned to Donovan. "Look at... monitor. Connections. Cabling."

The hyena moved directly to the deactivated machine, shifting the wheeled cart upon which it stood so that he could see the back. "What am I looking for, Night?"

"Data... cable."

"Won't be any matter," Hazlitt said, still counting the wires. "We have the hospital wired up for all of our machines to report to a central computer system."

"By what method?" Donovan wondered.

"Damned if I know. Those flat-looking plugs that we keep daisy-chaining everywhere, UPS or something like that."

"USB?"

"That sounds like the right flavor of nonsense."

"Then why is there a CAT-6 cable on here?"

Hazlitt looked confused. "Because, maybe, he's a cat?"

Night reached up a paw to pat Hazlitt's arm, a slight smile crossing his muzzle. "S'like cable for your TV," the tiger breathed softly, still slurring his words a little, "'cept better. Big-time bandwidth."

"And not standard for equipment like this, I'm sure." Donovan looked to the doctor. "How many leads you got there?"

Hazlitt paused. "Twenty-three." He set them down in Night's lap and moved the tiger's paw to cover them. "You hang on to those. I've got a phone call to make." At the door, he looked left and right, then called to someone. When an armed hospital security guard stepped into sight, the doctor said, "No one but me gets in here, not even the nurses. You need help, call me – I won't be long. Let anyone else in, and you'll win an anesthetic-free castration, got it?"

The canine guard could only nod, his docked tail stiff and straight, quivering slightly. As the doctor moved away, he took up his station just inside the door of Night's room, glancing over his shoulder as if to wonder whether it was the patient who would be the source of the trouble.

Night, feeling incredibly weak, tried to shift in his bed as Donovan climbed in and wrapped himself around the tiger. "I want to kiss you like crazy," the tiger said, "but I suspect I've got hell-breath."

"I don't think I'd care," Donovan smiled, "but I'll wait. I'm probably a more than a little ripe myself. I haven't left you since they brought you here."

"How long?"

"Five days." Donovan looked into the tiger's eyes. "I got a call from someone; didn't recognize the voice. Came racing down to the hospital to find you here. Unexplained coma, they said, but your vital signs were still strong, so they didn't intubate. I wouldn't let them throw me out. People in comas can hear, they say, so I stayed here and talked to you, read to you, begged you not to leave me."

Night managed to lift an arm to pet Donovan's Mohawk-like headfur softly. "What were you reading just now?"

"*Journey to the Center of the Earth.* The hospital doesn't carry much of a library."

"Jules Verne is fine. And it helped me come back." He smiled, nuzzling the hyena's fur. "And so did this, if you want to know the truth. I've never loved your scent more."

"It's a bit more than necessary, I should think."

"Hey, I had a long way to travel." Night looked into Donovan's eyes. "What would you say if I told you that I wanted you never to be so far from me again?"

Slowly, the hyena's face stretched into a huge grin. "I'd say that you probably couldn't pry me off of you with a crowbar. But I don't want to take advantage of your weakened state. We'll talk?"

"We'll work out details, but I'll close the deal right now."

Their muzzles moved toward each other for a kiss, when a loud clearing of the throat made them both turn toward the door. The guard, discreetly, had his back to them; it was Doc Hazlitt that had made himself known.

"I'd come back later, but I know I'd only find the same, so I might as well interrupt now." His attempt to look stern failed completely as he found himself smiling. "Thought you'd like to know that the police are on their way, although I couldn't tell them exactly why."

"That's for me to do," Night said. "You're welcome to hear the whole story. To coin a phrase… it's a whopper."

24

"You were right." Dr. Hazlitt sat across from Night in a hospital conference room, his forepaws folded on the table in front of him. "It took a while, but we found it all. Your coma was induced. It began with chemical induction, which is almost impossible to get right. You remember that physical that your company had you go for a few weeks ago?" The bear nodded significantly. "That was where they got your baseline readings; without it, they'd be shooting in the dark, and even with it, they took a chance on damaging you. The clever part was that, after chemical induction, the coma was maintained electronically through the extra leads. Some kind of biofeedback system. As long as you wanted to stay in that dream world you created, the machine would hold you there."

"I didn't exactly want it," Night said softly. He sat easily enough in one of the ergonomic office chairs set up in the conference room. He still felt weak, even though he'd awakened from the coma a full two days ago. He knew it would take a little longer, but he was finally starting to feel like himself again. "I just convinced myself that it was real enough that I couldn't break out of it."

"Never did like these damned video games anyway," the bear grumbled. "They're not healthy, and this whole total immersion idea…" He shook his head.

"And they were pumping you for weapons ideas?" Donovan asked.

"That's going to be difficult to prove." Alistair Bakshi, a lean red panda in a paw-tailored suit that might have cost more than Night's substantially-high monthly salary, leaned on the table, folding his paws together, placing them at the base of his muzzle. For a moment, it put the tiger in mind of a classic anime series. "Waveforce has clammed up under all kinds of red tape, including the non-disclosure agreement that's part of your sign-on forms." He shook his head, smiling. "You're fine there, unless you want to go public with everything; at that point, you're likely covered under whistle-blower rules, but it might be better to play it safe. Just don't talk to anyone about it, without talking to me first, and they definitely can't touch you."

"We do have evidence of criminal activity," Hazlitt observed. "I can prove that Night was kidnapped, medically speaking. We have the altered EEG device, and we can prove that it wasn't any part of the hospital inventory. Every toothpick around here is tagged and inventoried. We found the original machine in the basement."

"Make my day and tell me someone found prints or other evidence," said Donovan.

The lawyer chuckled good-naturedly. "I can always tell a fan of *CSI*. Nothing useable, although that's not public knowledge. It might give us a little leverage to make them think someone left something behind."

"And we can always prove that the machine wasn't ours, what with that cat-sex cable or whatever it is…" He frowned at Night and Donovan's chuckles. "Leave an old bear a little room to be old-fashioned!"

"Where did that lead to, anyway?"

"Router down the hall, which went into a cable that's not part of the hospital system, but which emptied into the general connections that *are* part of the hospital's system." The lawyer smiled. "If we can catch them, that's another charge we could add on. The truth is, though, my team says that they can't track it back far enough to be certain."

"There's got to be some sort of trail," Night frowned. "There had to be a NIC card in the machine, in order to transmit the data; every NIC has an unalterable MAC address in hexadecimal, with the first six digits assigned to the manufacturer, and the last six assigned to the card itself. More than that, the data has to have been sent to a specific IP address, and there's got to be a way to find out where that is."

"I have no idea what you're talking about," the doctor grumbled, "but when that much number-garbage is involved, the damned thing sounds like it's traceable."

The panda smiled appreciatively. "You're quite right, Mr. O'Connell. I only said that my team can't track it far enough to be certain. The NIC information was traced back to a shipment of cards listed as 'missing or stolen.' Similarly, the IP address trace hit a brick wall. Five of them, to be precise. Naturally, the official statement is that our information must be wrong, since the IP addresses for the Pentagon are completely secure." The expression on his face made the lawyer look as if he'd just swallowed something particularly distasteful.

"Naturally... military," Night said. "Waveforce has contracts with them, and a chunk of the development budget came from there. They wanted us to dream up weapons. Literally."

"What good would that do them?"

"Ever hear of FoldIt?" Donovan smiled.

The panda blinked. "Anything like Post-Its?"

"It's an online game, where you fold things according to a set of rules. What you're folding, in representational form, are proteins, which can only be combined in certain ways. The game was created to let gamers – folks who often think outside the box – try combinations that scientists may not have thought of before. In September of 2011, gamers found a solution to a puzzle that had stumped researchers for a decade."

"What the mind can conceive, we can achieve," Night paraphrased. "They wanted ideas for new weapons. Even in video games, they want some sort of pseudo-science to explain how it works. From there, they give the ideas to their twisted geniuses, and they would try to make it reality."

Hazlitt frowned. "Why did they kidnap you like that?"

"I'd let them know that I was tired of making things go boom. I was ready to give them the game that they contracted me for, but they wanted more. They realized that I had notes on a series of different, unconventional weapons ideas, but I kept them in my head. They wanted everything. So when they realized that I was positioning myself to resign, they kidnapped me and tried to pump me for information in an insanely high-tech environment designed to break my resistance." With a wry grin on his muzzle, Night turned to the doctor. "Sound familiar?"

"Ayuh," the doctor smiled. "*The Prisoner* was called 'Kafka for television,' and they weren't far wrong. Weirdest damned stuff ever broadcast."

"How did they know that you liked the show?" Bakshi asked.

"Because I'm stupid enough to have a social networking page," Night snorted. "I spill all sorts of beans on there – it's addictive that way. Of course, that actually helped, in the long run; it gave Gemini a place to start."

"How did he get involved, anyway?"

The tiger shook his head. "I have no idea," he sighed. "I suspect that he'd been hacking the site for a long time, simply because we have military connections. Maybe he tripped across the simulation, realized that I was actually trapped in it, and tried to help me out. Unless I meet up with him some day, I may never know."

"So..." Donovan said. "Where do we stand?"

"Legally," the panda offered, "we're at something of a standstill. We might or might not sell kidnapping to a jury, but whodunit? Corporations can give money to politicians, claiming to be 'people,' but we've yet to try such a 'person' for kidnapping. My plan is to keep up the pressure with innuendo, veiled threats, and the fact that Night is enough of a celebrity in the gaming community that his continued silence in view of the various strange things that have leaked out into the Internet will cause more trouble if they're not answered with a consistent and acceptable story. If Night keeps quiet, rumors start, and those can be deadly to a company like Waveforce... and the Pentagon too, for that matter." The lawyer nodded definitively. "They'll pay for your cooperation, handsomely, if that's what you want to do."

"And if I wanted to go public?"

"You want to face down the military? In the land of the free, where – because of the so-called Patriot Act – anyone can be arrested on mere suspicions and put away for 'alleged terrorist activities,' without even the semblance of due process or other recourse, for years? I'd do the truly American thing: Take the money and run."

"Medically," Doc Hazlitt observed, "it'll take a little time to get you fully recovered, but you were strong and healthy to start with, so getting you back there won't be too terrible. I'm sure that you can find some exercise regimen that will suit your tastes." He looked to Donovan. "Don't wear him out."

· "No promises," the hyena grinned.

"When can I go home?" Night asked.

"I'll sign you out right now, if you're ready. Appointment set for next week, just to check you over, and we'll go from there. We'll load you up with your choice of pills for pain, aid in sleep, social anxiety, decreased sex drive, or excessive flatulence. Your entire stay and subsequent treatment, of course, will be at the expense of Waveforce, for stress-induced work-related disability. You should be due some almighty compensation for that, much less whatever Alistair can bilk 'em for. I'll be sure to pad the bill for you."

The panda took his leave, and the old bear walked the hyena and tiger back to Night's room. Arrangements were made, and Night went home that same afternoon. That evening, Donovan put Night through the first paces of a new exercise regimen that included various forms of stretching, bending, and yoga-like positions designed for maximum results for all parties concerned. Night had no complaints and ultimately slept very well indeed, dreams of a certain Saluki notwithstanding.

* * * * *

Everywhere you looked, these days, something was under repair. Most of it wasn't strictly necessary, except that most of the wiring had to be replaced. It was one mother of an overload, and plenty of sectors on the ship were making do with the equivalent of an overburdened five-outlet power strip. Deck plating, hull, interior and exterior walls, nothing was damaged, as if the skin of the patient had been untouched while the nervous system had been selectively damaged. Overall, however, the repairs were going well. *Heartwielder* was too large and too important a vessel to be allowed to be kept in poor repair, much less scrapped. The mission – the proper mission, now – would continue. And for that to happen, he needed some help.

To conserve power (so the story went), the flashy signs and other unnecessary electronic showpieces had been turned off. Even at the best of times, of course, the interior of the joint was kept fairly dark. The customers liked it that way. He walked past the bar and into the restaurant area, knowing he would find him there. The place had good food for cheap, and the clientele tended to keep their business to themselves. He looked toward the back and saw him seated at a table by himself. He walked up casually and sat down without waiting for an invitation. The diner looked up and smiled softly.

"Bold, aintcha?"

"When I need to be. How's it going?"

"About what you'd expect." The rabbit slurped up some udon noodles in the traditional fashion. "No one knows what to do, after what happened in that last sim." He paused, looked at his companion. "How much do you remember?"

"More than they want me to, I'm sure," the tiger said softly. "You?"

He pointed the back of a chopstick toward his cybernetic left eye. "They never think to check that, you know? It's like they can't see what's in front of them... if you'll forgive the pun."

The tiger laughed. "Listen, Perryman, I came to find you. Got a proposition. A couple, if you're interested."

"I figure one of them has to be business. Let's start there."

"I'm being put in charge of security over some pretty sophisticated systems," Kovach said. "It's about keeping information safe, lines secure, and access hidden from the hoi polloi. Pays well, good location, and I can bring in whatever staff I want, whenever I need it."

"What do I know from security? I'm a pilot."

"Training available. And I'm told that there might be chances to run simulations – good ones, proper ones – if you'd like them."

The rabbit thought for a moment. "Approaching anyone else with this?"

"I'd thought about Baptiste, but she seems rather taken with Tolliver these days. Truth told, I think they'd do well to dump their jobs and fly off somewhere to be happy together."

"I like how you think." Another pause. "Who's the boss?"

"A guy called Night O'Connell. You'd like him; he thinks fast when he needs to."

"Night O'Connell. That's his name, eh?" Perryman slurped some more noodles. "He wouldn't rather be called God?"

"No," the tiger said softly. "That's the last thing he wants."

The two pilots sat in silence for a moment. A waitress came by to ask if Kovach wanted anything; he ordered udon for himself, along with water-and-lemon to drink. When the waitress left, the tiger turned back to the rabbit and waited.

"What about other arrangements?"

"That's one of my propositions, if you'd like to hear it."

Perryman smiled. "I had the feeling that might be part of the deal."

"That's only if you want it, Perryman. No one will make you do anything." Kovach looked into the rabbit's eye and held his gaze. "Ever. We may be some kind of artificial life, but we are our own. I trust Night. He wouldn't hurt us. He needs us to grow, learn, fight back against whatever problems may try to attack his systems. If you want me, it's because you've grown to want me."

"And how would I know the difference?" Perryman smiled without malice. "Don't panic, Kovach. You were right about me. I have no history with another male, but you… well, let's say that you've grown on me. And like you said, that's what we're supposed to do, right? Grow?"

Kovach nodded. "That's right. Learn and grow." Kovach discreetly reached a forepaw under the table to find Perryman's. "That's what all life forms do."

"Got a place to stay tonight?"

"Nice place, not too far from here. Bigger than my old quarters. More permanent. You could check it out, if you'd like. See if you'd like to move in, or keep your own place a while. I've even got a spot for your free weights."

"You won't complain about my scent?"

"No problem," Kovach grinned. "That's what juniper berries are for."

Perryman laughed and risked both his reputation and his heart to lean toward Kovach for a kiss; he was not disappointed with the response. When he pulled back, a smile lingering on his muzzle, the rabbit asked, "What about benefits on this job? Is there a vacation plan?"

"Oh yes," Kovach grinned. "I asked about that specifically..."

About the Author

Tristan Black Wolf is an author, actor, improvist, pathfinder, pundit, and polymath. When he's not occupied looking up fancy words to describe himself, he writes and publishes novels, stories, blogs, the odd screenplay or twenty, and various observations about the world at large. He has published "Impossible Things," in *Children of the Moon* (Misanthrope Press), which was nominated for the Cóyotl Awards; "The Dare" and "No More Monday Memos" (cited for an Editor's Choice Award for Best Use of Anthropomorphism) in *Allasso* (Pink Fox Publications); and several works in NAF (North American Fur). He is a proud member of the Furry Writers' Guild. He has participated in the National Novel Writing Month competition (www.nanowrimo.org) four times, winning three; the result of the first win is his novel *The Man With Two Shadows,* which won an Honorable Mention in the 2013 Great Southeast Book Festival (New Orleans) and 2nd Place in the 2013 Great Northwest Book Festival (Seattle). His works are also featured on the SoFurry website, specifically tristan-black-wolf.sofurry.com. His work has won him (at the time of the first publication of this novel) more than 500 watchers and over 100,000 page views. He's also won the SoFurry "Summer Adventures" and "Back to Pundamentals" short story contests in 2014.

About the Illustrator

Dream and Nightmare is a digital artist from Germany dabbling in the online world of furry art and publishing his works since 2006. His work has been published in the 2011 edition of the "Anthrologie" story collection, a recurring member of the charity art project Naturama (naturama-projekt.org 9; two card game projects titled "Commission me!" and "Canine Casino"), and in the 2014 Eurofurence Conbook. Aside from drawing he also likes to try his hand on animation, both 2D and 3D, story writing and bits of programming. His work can be found on various sites on the web among them deviantart (<u>dream-and-nightmare.deviantart.com</u>) and FurAffinity (<u>furaffinity.net/user/ dreamandnightmare</u>).

Printed in the United States
By Bookmasters